A Country
Cotillion

Elizabeth dreamed that night. She was lying naked in her bed, and *he* was there, his hair the brightest of gold in the glow from a lantern. He wore a long silk robe that was tied loosely at the waist, and he smiled as he came toward her. The robe slid softly to the floor, and she gazed at his body, so lean, bronzed, and beautiful. But as she reached up to him, his face changed, and it was no longer her late husband, James French, who came to her, who joined her in her bed, his body warm and firm, his lips teasing and arousing – but instead there was the stranger whose name she did not even know . . . the stranger who woke in her a desire that could only bring disaster outside the world of dreams. . . .

A Country Cotillion

Sandra Heath

ROBERT HALE · LONDON

ISBN 978-0-7090-8659-8

Robert Hale Limited
Clerkenwell House
Clerkenwell Green
London EC1R 0HT

www.halebooks.com

2 4 6 8 10 9 7 5 3 1

Typeset in 11½/16½pt Palatino
by Derek Doyle & Associates, Shaw Heath
Printed and bound in Great Britain
by the MPG Books Group

CHAPTER 1

WHEN YOUNG WIDOW Elizabeth French set off for the Duke of Devonshire's grand January ball with handsome Sir Alexander Norrington, to whom she was about to be betrothed, she had no idea at all that before the ball was over her hitherto reasonably settled existence would have received a very disagreeable jolt. Her life was going to take a very different path from the one at present mapped out, but as Alexander's town carriage left Oakgrove House, her villa in Kensington, that bitterly cold winter evening in 1814, there was no hint of what the night held in store.

Elizabeth shivered a little, even though she was enveloped in a fur-lined gray velvet cloak, and beneath her feet there rested a hot brick wrapped in cloth. She had never known cold such as this, and although there had not been any snow as yet, everyone knew that it would come before long. It was being said that if the freezing temperatures continued, the Thames itself would ice over, as it had done several times in the past.

The carriage left the villa's curving drive, and entered the narrow tree-lined lane that led to the main London turnpike road. Elizabeth glanced out a little apprehensively, for foot-pads and highwaymen had been at work in recent weeks. Several of her neighbors had been robbed, and their complaints to the authorities had been strenuous enough to result in an extra patrol of the watch taking place. There hadn't been any further robberies, but neither had any of the miscreants been arrested, and so she was understandably uneasy until the carriage emerged from the confines of the lane and then turned east along the broad expanse of the highway.

As the buildings of Kensington village passed by, Elizabeth leaned her head back against the carriage's brown leather upholstery. She was twenty-four years old, with soft gray eyes, long, dark-blond curls, and a peaches-and-cream complexion. Beneath her cloak her tiny-waisted figure was dainty in a sleeveless apricot satin slip and short-sleeved overgown of shimmering gold-spotted plowman's gauze. The overgown was high-waisted, with a drawstring immediately beneath her breasts, and her skirts reached just to her ankles, as was the latest fashion, so that her little golden brocade slippers were always visible.

Her thick hair was twisted up into a knot from which a single heavy ringlet fell to the nape of her neck, and small curls framed her heart-shaped face. The only jewelry she wore was a pair of exquisite golden earrings given to her by her late parents, who had died in a carriage overturn while she had been far away in Madras, finding out the painful truth about her husband, James French.

Elizabeth lowered her gaze to the spangled reticule and folded fan lying on her lap. James had begun to intrude a great deal upon her thoughts in recent days, even though his womanizing and increasing cruelty had eventually made their marriage deeply unhappy. It was of their early days together that she found herself thinking most, days when she had been swept off her foolish feet by his dashing golden-haired good looks and devastating charm.

Oh, what a lover he had been. He had been a master of his art, and she, adoring him so very much, had been an eager and willing pupil. He had awakened her to sensual joys she had not dreamed existed and he made her feel that she was all that mattered in the world. Little fool that she had been, she had believed that the happiness would go on forever, and that they would never cease to love each other as they had in the beginning. She had been taken in, and in the end she had paid the price of her folly, but for a while, a sweet period of ecstasy, she had known the sort of love that many passed through their entire lives without knowing at all.

Kensington was slipping away behind now, and the carriage was driving on toward Knightsbridge. Elizabeth's thoughts were not of the Devonshire House ball, but of James, and the casual event that had brought him back into her thoughts. It had been pure chance that had taken her carriage through Hanover Square when she had been on her way to visit her Aunt Avery in Park Lane. When they had first been married, she and James had taken a house in the square, and something made her order the coachman to draw up by the railing of the octagonal garden in the center of Mayfair's oldest quadrangle.

The house was now occupied by an eminent lawyer, and like all the others in the square was built of red brick, with three main stories, a basement, and an attic. It stood near the northwest corner, looking south toward George Street and St. George's Church, where she and James had been married, and it still had the same dark-green door and lion's head knocker.

She had gazed at the door, remembering the times when she and James had entered or left, smiling and laughing together. She remembered one morning in particular, the morning when he had gone to East India House in Leadenhall Street, to arrange their passage to Madras. They had awoken very late, and it had been even later before they had eventually gone down to breakfast in the little room overlooking the gardens at the rear of the house. She had worn a pretty pink floral wrap with thick lace spilling from the wrists, and her hair had been brushed loose, just as James had liked it. He was going alone to Leadenhall Street, and so had already been dressed to go out, in an olive-green coat and cream cord breeches. His waistcoat had been made of a particularly stylish oyster brocade, and his voluminous neckcloth had sported a pin with a single, very large pearl. His golden hair had been tousled, for it always defied the efforts of a comb, and his deep-blue eyes had been lazily quizzical as he looked at her across the white-clothed table.

'Are you sure you wish to remove to faraway Madras?' His voice had been light and soft, with a hint of a Scottish accent.

'I will go anywhere with you, James.'

'I do not have to take up this position with the East India Company.'

'But you wish to.'

He nodded. 'Yes, I wish to.'

She remembered teasing him a little. 'You have a notion to become a nabob, do you not?'

'I fully intend to, so it is no notion.'

'Well, I have a notion to become a nabob's wife, a nabobana, or whatever such ladies are called.'

'A nabobess, I believe.'

'That then.'

He smiled. 'You will have Madras society at your feet, my darling.'

'I will not notice anyone but you.' She had met his eyes then, loving him so much that it was like a pain aching through her.

'Look at me like that, and I will be obliged to return you promptly to the bed, wench,' he murmured, tossing down his napkin and getting up. 'And if that happens, I will be late for my appointment.'

He came around the table to kiss her. His arms had slipped lovingly around her from behind, and his lips had brushed her cheeks and her hair before he had gone out. She remembered hearing him speak briefly to the butler, who had given him his hat, gloves, and cane. A moment later the carriage had driven away toward distant Leadenhall Street.

Gazing at the past from the more sober present, Elizabeth had been so lost in thought as she gazed at that remembered Hanover Square door, that she had given quite a start when it had opened, and a tall, elegant gentleman had emerged. He had paused on the step to take his leave of the lawyer whose house it now was, and she had found herself staring once again at the husband she had loved so much, but had now lost forever.

The gentleman on the doorstep not only wore a green coat and cream breeches, but he had golden hair that was as unruly and eyecatching as James's had been. He was also the same height and build, with broad shoulders and slender hips.

The illusion had been so real that she had sat forward, her trembling hand reaching out toward the handle of the carriage door. 'James? Oh, James, can it be you?' The foolish, longing words had slipped so easily from her lips that she suddenly knew how very much she missed those early days together, and how much she still loved James as he had been then. Tears had sprung to her eyes as she realized that it could not possibly be him.

She had watched as the stranger put on his hat and gloves and then went to climb into the curricle that waited for him at the curb. He took up the reins and flung the restive team forward, so that the little vehicle skimmed around the cobbled square, passing right by her. She saw his face very clearly then. He was very like James, just as dashing and breathtakingly handsome, with keen blue eyes and a firm mouth with fine lips. His complexion was tanned from much time spent in the open air, and his features were rugged and yet aristocratic. She had no doubt that whoever he was he was of noble birth, and that he was no languid drawing-room knight, but a man of action and swift decision.

She still did not know who he was, but it was because of him that she was now doubtful about her future with Alexander. Seeing that golden-haired gentleman leave the house in Hanover Square had forced her to remember the way it had once been with James, and to face the fact that the love she shared now with Alexander would never match what she had known then.

The carriage was now driving through Knightsbridge, and she stole a secret glance at him as he sat opposite. With him there had never been the same fire and excitement, but then he would never play her false a thousand times over with any woman who caught his roving eye. It had been because he was unlike James that in the beginning she had allowed him to woo her. The pain of James's deceits and infidelities had been fresh, and she did not want to be reminded. Alexander did not remind her at all. He was steadfast and easygoing, kind and gentle, and he adored her with all his heart. But his kisses did not turn her blood to fire in her veins, and his caresses did not arouse the passionate desire that flared into life when James's hand had touched hers.

She felt guilty and disloyal as she glanced at him in the light from a passing street lamp. He was not as good-looking as James had been, or indeed as the stranger in Hanover Square was, but he was very attractive for all that. He was tall and slender, with thick dark-brown hair and long-lashed hazel eyes, his lips were full and sensitive, and he was naturally a little pale, all of which led to his being regarded by many of the more impressionable ladies as being the embodiment of Lord Byron's romantic hero, Childe Harold.

Childe Harold's Pilgrimage had been published almost two years before, and had taken society by storm. Lord Byron was the object of much adulation, and his hero of much female fluttering and improper longing. Poor Alexander was a little tired of being called 'Harold' by his teasing male friends, and was now wont to respond by pointing out a little sharply that he did not possess any dark secrets, nor was he prey to unmentionable vice.

Tonight he did not resemble a wandering medieval knight, but was very much the up-to-date London man of fashion. Beneath his astrakhan-collared fawn greatcoat he wore a

11

silver-buttoned black velvet evening coat that was deliberately cut too tight to be buttoned, so that his white satin waistcoat and lace-trimmed shirt front could be shown off to best
advantage. His superbly tailored white silk pantaloons made
the most of his long legs, and his full, starched cravat was
finished with a glittering diamond pin. He was wealthy,
sought after, and very eligible indeed, but although he could
have had his pick of brides, it had been James French's widow
who had caught his eye from the moment she had returned to
London and purchased the villa in Kensington.

He had laid siege to her, dancing constant and determined
attendance, and proving himself time and time again to be
everything her husband had not been. His patience had
finally paid dividend, and at Christmas she had accepted his
proposal. In a month's time, on his twenty-ninth birthday,
their formal betrothal would take place at his residence,
Norrington House, Cavendish Square, and on the first day of
May she would become Lady Norrington at a wedding cere-
mony at the same church where once she had become Mrs
James French.

The carriage had now entered Piccadilly, which was almost
as busy at night as it was during the day. The shops, hotels,
stagecoach ticket offices, residences, and lodging houses were
all still brightly lit, and the pavements were crowded with
people. Devonshire House was not far ahead now, and once
again Elizabeth endeavored to push all thoughts of the past
into the background, where they belonged. But events were
already in train that were to make it very difficult indeed for
her to ignore what had once been.

The night would probably have passed without event had
it not been decided that the ball was the perfect occasion for

the first appearance in society of Elizabeth's spoiled, romanti-
cally impressionable young cousin, Lady Isobel Crawford.
Isobel was eighteen years old, with shining chestnut hair,
large green eyes, and a willowy figure that always looked
particularly enchanting in clinging muslin gowns.

Isobel was the only child of Elizabeth's uncle and aunt, the
Earl and Countess of Southwell, who had had her late in life
and who consequently had always indulged her every whim.
The earl had been in poor health for some time now, and he
and Elizabeth's aunt seldom left Southwell Park, their fine
country seat near Nottingham, so that when Isobel was old
enough to enter London society, she was sent to reside in Park
Lane with her Aunt Avery. Isobel had traveled south very
eagerly indeed, for she had read and reread *Childe Harold's
Pilgrimage* and longed to meet exciting Lord Byron, whose
estate at Newstead Abbey was tantalizingly close to
Southwell Park, but who infuriatingly chose to live in the
capital.

When she had arrived in Park Lane, society gossip was
such that she was determined at all costs to make the acquaintance of the poet, who was said to be as handsome, fascinating, and fatalistic as the hero he created. At length she had
met him at one of her aunt's private dinner parties, but he had
scorned her, and had remarked within her hearing that he
found her tedious and tiresome. Isobel's adoration had been
crushed in a moment, but she had very swiftly perceived how
best to prick his arrogant vanity. Knowing that he had a very
high opinion of his good looks, but was unfortunately cursed
with a club foot, she remarked, within his hearing, that he
would not ever have the grace to dance well. She was
rewarded by the angry color that had stained his face, and by

his early departure from the dinner party. But although she now disliked him intensely, she still could not help admiring his poetry, especially *Childe Harold's Pilgrimage*, and she consoled herself that somewhere in London there was bound to be a gentleman who would become her Harold, her pale handsome hero.

It was to be upon Alexander that her covetous, longing gaze would fall, but as she traveled to Devonshire House with her aunt, he was still no more than a name to her. She and Elizabeth had never been particularly close. As children the five years between them had been too great, and then Elizabeth had married and left England. They had met several times at Aunt Avery's, but had not had a great deal to say to each other, and the identity of Elizabeth's future husband was a matter of indifference to Isobel. Her only concern about the forthcoming betrothal ball and subsequent wedding was that both occasions would give her an opportunity to dress in her finest clothes, and shine to excellent advantage.

Devonshire House, which faced across Piccadilly toward Green Park, was a rather ugly mansion set behind a high brick wall. The ball was such an important occasion that all the nearby streets were choked with fine carriages, and a small army of liveried footmen was required to keep at bay the crowds of onlookers who braved the icy winter night to watch the *haut ton* in all its luxury.

The house was approached through wide wooden gates that opened into a courtyard, and the main entrance was beneath a plain pillared carriage porch. From the porch, the guests stepped into a vast hall at the far end of which there was a semicircular bay overlooking the lawns and the famous elm trees that in summer gave such leafy shade. The bay also contained a circular staircase made of marble and alabaster, with a baluster of gilded ironwork and a solid crystal handrail, and the duke's glittering guests ascended this to the ballroom on the floor above.

The whole building was ablaze with lights, one of the most fashionable orchestras in the land had been engaged to play, Gunter's of Berkeley Square had provided one of their matchless ball suppers, and there was a lavish supply of chilled champagne and lime cup. Every room was filled to overflowing with hothouse flowers, as if it were the height of summer instead of one of the coldest winters in living memory, but the weather wasn't on anyone's mind as the *beau monde* danced the night away.

William George Spencer Cavendish, sixth Duke of Devonshire, was twenty-six and a bachelor, but he was also a very lavish host, and the ball had been a resounding success from the outset. It became even more of a success when the duke himself introduced a bold new cotillion. Cotillions had been in favor for a long time now, but this new version, called *L'Échange*, involved sets of only two couples, and ended rather wickedly with an exchange of partners and a kiss on the lips. The opportunity for flirtation and intrigue was manifest, as the duke's delighted guests were not slow to perceive.

By the time midnight arrived, Elizabeth and Isobel had been at the ball for several hours, but although they had encountered each other when Elizabeth had come to pay her respects to Aunt Avery, Alexander had not been present because he had gone to speak for a while with his old friend, Tom Crichton.

As the chimes of the witching hour died away, it was not

the new cotillion that was in progress, but a stately *ländler*. A sea of elegant, bejeweled people swayed beneath the shimmering chandeliers of the white, blue, and gold ballroom where paintings by Veronese and Rubens alternated with vast mirrors, and the babble of conversation sometimes drowned the sound of the orchestra as it played on the dais at the far end of the room.

Isobel was stealing a few minutes to herself, and had taken refuge in a corner where a red velvet sofa was almost hidden by an arrangement of flowers, ferns, and potted palms. She had danced virtually every dance, been flattered and admired by countless gentlemen, but there had not been one who had even begun to turn her head. She snapped open her fan, and wafted it discontentedly before her face. She wore a delicate white muslin gown that outlined every curve of her figure, and there were diamonds at her throat and in her hair.

As the *ländler* proceeded, her gaze moved idly over the dancers, coming to rest suddenly upon her cousin Elizabeth. The gaze immediately became critical, taking in every inch of Elizabeth's appearance, and conceding a little reluctantly that the apricot satin and plowman's gauze became her very well indeed.

Then, at last, Isobel's glance moved on to the gentleman with whom her cousin was dancing. Her heart stood still as she saw his pale, romantic face, his thick dark hair, and his thoughtful hazel eyes. It was Childe Harold. Her fan became still, and for a moment she was deaf to the sounds of the ball. She heard her heart begin to beat again, and then the strains of the orchestra became audible once more. Who was he? She had to meet him!

A flush appeared on her cheeks, and a new light shone in her green eyes as she rose slowly to her feet. She had found her Childe Harold, now she meant to win him.

CHAPTER 2

LORD JUSTIN FANSHAW was a chinless, freckled young man with protruding teeth and receding sandy hair. He had worshipped Isobel from the moment she entered the ballroom, and now his eyes brightened as he saw her approaching.

'Lady Isobel?'

'Lord Justin.'

'Would . . . would you care for some lime cup?' he asked.

'That would be most agreeable,' she replied, allowing him to conduct her to one of the many sofas arranged around the edge of the ballroom.

She sat down, still watching the *ländler* as a glass of the cup was procured from a footman's tray. She waited until Lord Justin had sat down next to her, before she nodded toward Elizabeth and her partner. 'Lord Justin, who is the gentleman dancing with my cousin Elizabeth?'

'Your cousin?' He searched the crowded floor. 'Ah, yes. She is with Sir Alexander Norrington, Lady Isobel.'

Sir Alexander? The man she was to marry? Isobel's heart sank with quick disappointment. So her Childe Harold was not unattached and free, but would soon make Elizabeth his bride.

Lord Justin was curious. 'I confess I find it a little strange that you do not know Sir Alexander, Lady Isobel. After all, if he is about to be betrothed to your cousin. . . ?'

'It is just that I have not yet been introduced to him,' Isobel replied. 'Elizabeth and I have not seen a great deal of each other since I have come to London. All I know is that it is to be a love match.'

'A love match? Yes, so I understand, although when I think of the lady's first marriage . . .' Lord Justin coughed a little awkwardly, for he had almost been indiscreet.

Isobel looked quickly at him. 'Yes? Do go on, sir.'

'Well, it isn't any of my business, Lady Isobel.'

'Please say what was on the tip of your tongue, Lord Justin.'

'It's just that I was acquainted with your cousin's first husband, James French, indeed I attended their wedding. They were so very happy together, and I thought them the perfect match, but it seems that James was not the fellow I took him for.'

'My aunt told me that James French turned out to be a wicked rakehell, Lord Justin.'

'Eh? Er – yes, he did, although it did not seem that way in the beginning. That was what I was about to say, for when I observe the lady with Sir Alexander, and then recall how it was when she was with James, I simply cannot believe . . .'

'Yes?' Isobel prompted.

'Really, Lady Isobel, I should not say anything more. I fear I may have consumed one glass of champagne too many.'

'I'm sure you haven't, sir,' Isobel answered quickly, anxious to find out more. 'What is it that you cannot believe about my cousin?'

'That she is as in love with Sir Alexander as he is with her.'

'Do you really doubt on that score, Lord Justin?'

'Look, I've said more than I should. Please forget that I've said anything at all, Lady Isobel.' He was now very uncomfortable indeed.

She smiled. 'But I will not say anything to anyone, Lord Justin. I promise to be all that is discreet.'

He look adoringly at her. 'Oh, I'm sure you will, Lady Isobel,' he said.

Her glance returned to the dancing, and to Elizabeth and Alexander. If what Lord Justin said was true, and Elizabeth did not return Alexander's love as she should, then might there not be a chance that the betrothal would never take place?

The *ländler* came to an end, and Elizabeth and Alexander left the floor, evidently not intending to join the next dance. Chance took them to a nearby sofa, but Elizabeth did not detect her young cousin's intense interest.

The master-of-ceremonies announced the new cotillion again, and there was a ripple of applause, for there wasn't a person present who did not enjoy *L'Échange*. A smile began to play upon Isobel's lips. *L'Échange*, with its change of partners and kiss on the lips, was the perfect way of not only meeting Sir Alexander Norrington, but of meeting him in a very exciting and romantic way!

She turned suddenly to Lord Justin. 'I would very much like to dance, sir.'

'Eh? Oh, yes, rather. Anything you wish, Lady Isobel,' he replied, relieving her of her glass and then getting up.

As he held out his white-gloved hand, she glanced again toward Elizabeth. 'Shall we invite my cousin and Sir Alexander to form the other half of our set?' she suggested.

He looked a little uncomfortable again. 'By all means, Lady Isobel, but you will bear in mind that everything I said to you was in the strictest confidence?'

'Of course.' She smiled.

Elizabeth looked up as they reached the sofa, and she was a little taken aback to see the warm smile on Isobel's lips. 'Why, good evening again, Isobel,' she murmured.

'Hello, Elizabeth. Lord Justin and I were hoping that you and Sir Alexander would join us for the new cotillion.' Isobel was able to look into Alexander's eyes at last, and her heart seemed to skip a beat. Close to her he was even more as she perceived Childe Harold, and she secretly crossed her fingers that Elizabeth would agree to the dance. In a few minutes now the shocking new cotillion might sweep her into this man's arms, and bring her lips to his. . . .

Elizabeth was a little puzzled as to why her cousin would wish them to dance, for until now Isobel could not have been less interested in her. 'Actually, Isobel, we thought we would sit this dance out.'

'Oh, please don't do that.' Isobel turned to Alexander. 'Please join us,' she begged, her lovely green eyes luminous and beseeching.

He succumbed. 'Of course we will,' he replied, smiling down at Elizabeth. 'One more measure, my love?'

She returned the smile. 'Oh, very well,' she agreed, accepting the hand he extended.

The two couples made their way through the crush to a

small space, and took up their positions just as the orchestra prepared to strike up. Isobel's whole body was now trembling with expectation. Soon she would feel his arms around her, and he would kiss her on the lips.

The orchestra began to play, and the sea of dancers twisted and turned to the jaunty melody. Cotillions were so named because of the swirling of the ladies' skirts, and *L'Échange* involved a great deal of such swirling. Isobel knew that she looked exquisite as she danced, and that the clinging white muslin of her gown outlined her willowy figure to perfection. Handkerchief favors were given and forfeited, hands touched, the gentlemen's arms rested briefly around their ladies' waists, and there was a great deal of laughter and amusement as the guests endeavored to remember the complicated measure.

L'Échange drew toward its diverting conclusion, and as the final bars rang out there was much merriment as the ladies twisted and twirled toward their new partners, who took them in their arms and kissed them on the lips.

Isobel was almost weak with anticipation as Alexander took her hands and drew her toward him. She closed her eyes, and her lips were soft and pliable beneath his. She longed to slip her arms around him, to embrace him passionately in front of everyone, but she knew that that would be a *faux pas* of the highest order. And so instead she savored the few brief seconds of intimacy, and as he released her she knew her fate had been sealed. This was the only man for her, and if she could win him for herself, then she would. He was her Childe Harold, and Elizabeth was not the bride for him.

Elizabeth was relieved when Lord Justin let her go, for not

only was he a clumsy dancer, but his kiss was so enthusiastic that his protruding teeth dug into her lips. As both couples left the floor, Isobel turned smilingly to her cousin. 'Elizabeth, we've hardly seen each other since I came to town, and I would so like to talk to you. May I call soon?'

Elizabeth was astonished. Isobel wished to call upon her? 'Yes, of course. Please call whenever you wish.'

'Oh, thank you.' Isobel looked at Alexander again. 'Why, I do believe that in the rush of joining the dance, you and I were not properly introduced, Sir Alexander.'

Elizabeth gave a brief laugh. 'Isobel, this is Sir Alexander Norrington. Alexander, my cousin, Lady Isobel Crawford.'

He took Isobel's hand and raised it to his lips. 'I am delighted to make your acquaintance, Lady Isobel.'

'And I yours, Sir Alexander,' she replied, giving him a shy smile. 'How very shocking that we should have danced such a scandalous dance without a formal introduction.'

'Shocking indeed,' he murmured, returning the smile.

She knew she had prolonged the moment as long as she could, and so reluctantly allowed Lord Justin to escort her back to their sofa, but she glanced back over her shoulder, anxious to look at Alexander as much as she could. He was everything she had ever dreamed of, and she wanted him desperately.

Alexander knew nothing of Isobel's interest, for his attention was on Elizabeth. 'The master-of-ceremonies has announced a polonaise. Would you like to dance again?'

'I think not, for my feet begin to ache from all the tripping around. Let us go to the supper room and sample some of Gunter's fare. Maybe we will be able to find a quiet corner.'

'Quiet corners are at a premium here tonight, but we will

see what we can find,' he replied, taking her hand and drawing it over the black velvet of his sleeve.

They found an unoccupied sofa by the entrance of the supper room, and sat down to enjoy a glass of chilled champagne, and a little of Mr Gunter's excellent cold chicken salad. After a moment Alexander mentioned Isobel again.

'Tell me, are all the ladies in your family as lovely as you and your cousin?'

'From which question I take it that Isobel meets with your approval?'

'How could I not find her enchanting?'

Elizabeth pursed her lips philosophically for a moment. 'Well, I have to concede that on tonight's performance she is indeed very engaging, but I also have to say that this Isobel is rather different from the one I've encountered hitherto. The other Isobel was a spoiled brat as a child, and hasn't seemed much better as an adult. She is quite carried away by all things romantic. My aunt tells me that she reads *Childe Harold's Pilgrimage* all the time, and that she was infatuated with Lord Byron until he was inexcusably rude to her one night.'

'Poor Lady Isobel.'

'Poor Lady Isobel gave as good as she got, from all accounts, and left his lordship smarting over his inability to dance.'

'Good for her. He needs taking down a peg or three,' Alexander replied with feeling. 'He certainly is not the sort of fellow I would approve of for Lady Isobel.'

'I agree, indeed I've been hearing some very shocking whispers about his dealings with his half-sister, Mrs Leigh.'

Alexander pretended to be appalled. 'Madam, you should

not know about such things.'

'But I'm a woman of the world, sir, a widow no less, and so I am permitted to know about such things.'

'It still isn't seemly.'

She grinned at him. 'You're right, of course, so I will not tell you everything I've heard about Lord Byron and Mrs Leigh.'

He was intrigued. 'What, exactly, have you heard?'

'Oh, I cannot possibly shock you by saying, sir.'

He smiled. 'You're a wretch, Elizabeth French.'

'I know.'

A footman came to take away their empty plates and to replenish their glasses of champagne. When Elizabeth spoke again it was of something else entirely.

'What were you and Tom Crichton so engrossed about earlier?'

'It seems Marcus Sheridan may be back in England.'

She looked blankly at him. 'Is that supposed to convey something to me? Who is Marcus Sheridan?'

'To give him his full title, he is Marcus Jonathan Philip Louis Sheridan, eighth Duke of Arlingham, Lord Rainford, and Baron de Valence of Princeleigh.'

'Good heavens, how very impressive.' Then her brows drew together. 'Duke of Arlingham? But I thought the line died out a year or so ago.'

'Marcus's father, the seventh duke, died not long ago, but the line itself most definitely did not. Marcus and his father did not get on at all, something about the old man never forgiving him for his mother's death giving birth to him. Anyway, they were always virtually at daggers drawn, and in the end Marcus couldn't endure it anymore. He upped and took himself off to America about ten years ago, and no one heard from him again.'

'Until now.'

'So it seems. Ten years is a long time, and although Marcus, Tom Crichton, and I were inseparable at Cambridge, it's difficult to be certain of recognizing someone again, especially if that person does not respond when hailed. Tom was driving his cabriolet out of Knightsbridge toward Kensington when he saw a horseman riding toward Mayfair. Now, I realize that Tom is often in his cups when he goes home at night, but he swears that this time he was quite sober. He is certain that the other fellow was Marcus, but although he called out to him, there was no reply, indeed he thinks the man increased his speed in order to avoid speaking. It's very curious.'

'Perhaps the man didn't hear Tom calling.'

'Tom is certain he did.'

Elizabeth shrugged a little. 'If it *was* Marcus, why would he ignore an old friend?'

'I have no idea at all, but as I've already said, ten years is a long time, and the Lord knows what Marcus is like now. He was always something of a tearaway, and could be the very devil with the fair sex, but then with looks like his he could hardly fail. Anyway, Tom hasn't left any stones unturned, and has made inquiries all around, but no one knows anything about Marcus being back here or not. Tom has even sent a letter to Rainworth Priory, in case Marcus has gone there.'

'I thought Rainworth was sold after the old duke's death,' Elizabeth replied.

He looked at her in some surprise, and then smiled. 'Of course, you would hear about Rainworth through Lady Isobel and her family, for it isn't far from Southwell Park, is it?'

'About seven miles. Rainworth is in the heart of Sherwood

Forest, Southwell Park is on the edge. Anyway, it was my uncle who thought the priory had been sold. It seems there were notices up to the effect that it was for sale, but that then they were taken down again. No one moved in, but everyone believed it was sold. All the staff are still there, I gather.'

'It's possible that Marcus sold it, I really wouldn't know.' Alexander sipped his champagne. 'Oh, it would be good to see him again.'

'Then I hope that you and Tom Crichton run him to earth.'

They looked up at that moment, because Isobel came hurrying in to find them. She was the picture of flusterment and charming apology, pausing to bite her lip for a moment before addressing Elizabeth.

'Elizabeth, I'm afraid I've taken rather a liberty, but I didn't think you'd mind.'

'What liberty?'

'Well, Aunt Avery has a headache and has left, but I wanted to stay, and so I told her a little fib. I said that you had offered to take me home should she decide to leave early.' Isobel lowered her eyes guiltily. 'I know I should not have said it, but I'm enjoying the ball so much that I couldn't bear to go just yet.'

Alexander had risen to his feet the moment she joined them, and he was now at immediate pains to reassure her. 'Lady Isobel, please do not think anything more of it. We would be delighted to take you home.'

'Oh, thank you. You're very kind and understanding, Sir Alexander,' Isobel breathed.

He smiled.

CHAPTER 3

THE DUKE OF Devonshire's guests departed as the first gray light of dawn marked the January sky. Occasional snowflakes drifted in the frozen air, as they had from time to time in recent days, and it was so cold that the crowds of onlookers had long since retired to the warmth of their homes.

London was quiet as Alexander's carriage drove west along an almost deserted Piccadilly, *en route* first for Park Lane, to take Isobel home to Aunt Avery's house, and then for Kensington, and Oakgrove House. There was no conversation in the carriage, they were all too tired for that, but Isobel hummed softly to herself as she gazed out at the empty pavements. The tune she chose was the melody from *L'Échange*, and it wasn't the London scene that she saw, but the dance floor at Devonshire House, and Childe Harold as he took her in his arms to kiss her on the lips.

She sat opposite Elizabeth and Alexander, looking lovely in a hooded white swansdown cloak that was trimmed at the front with little red satin bows. The soft swansdown framed her face, and her hair and tiara were not entirely concealed, so that her diamonds sparkled and flashed in the light from passing street lamps. She had seldom left her cousin's side since confessing to having fibbed to Aunt Avery, and thus she had managed to spend a great deal of time in Alexander's company. Each moment with him had served to reinforce her desire to win him, for there was something about him that captured her imagination. When she looked at his pale face, she saw a melancholy soul in need of her comfort, and when she imagined a shadow in his eyes, she thought of dark secrets bravely borne. She reminded herself of what Lord Justin had said, and told herself that her cousin Elizabeth was not as deeply in love with Alexander as she should be. If Elizabeth's heart were not fully committed to the forthcoming betrothal, then was it so wrong to set out to break the relationship by stealing the prospective bridegroom? No, it wasn't wrong at all, in fact it was almost justified. Isobel continued to hum *L'Échange*, a tune that was particularly appropriate to her situation, for just as the shocking new cotillion concluded with a change of partner, so she meant to see to it that Sir Alexander Norrington changed partners as well, from Mrs Elizabeth French to Lady Isobel Crawford.

The carriage approached Hyde Park and the corner of Park Lane, and as it slowly turned north out of Piccadilly, Alexander spoke suddenly to Elizabeth. 'I've been thinking that it would be very agreeable if we paid a brief visit to my mother and sister at Norrington Court. It's been some time since we saw them, and my mother has been plaguing me with invitations. I know it's a long way to Lincolnshire, but we have time to accomplish a stay there before the betrothal ball requires us to come back to London. What do you say? Shall we go?'

Elizabeth was caught a little off guard by the sudden

invitation. Go to Lincolnshire with the betrothal day so near? There was so much to still arrange for the celebratory ball. . . . But at the same time, it would be very pleasant indeed to see his mother and sister again, especially at Norrington Court, which was a very beautiful old house that had originally been built as a medieval castle. The Norringtons had been lords of Norrington manor since the time of the Norman conquest, and were well loved and respected in that part of Lincolnshire. The atmosphere was always soothing and comfortable, and the company very pleasing indeed. She smiled at him, her gray eyes warm in the gloom of the carriage.

'I would love to go,' she replied.

He drew her hand to his lips. 'I will make the arrangements without delay. We will leave well within the week.'

Opposite them, Isobel's humming had stopped. The last thing she wanted was for Alexander to leave London. She leaned urgently toward Elizabeth. 'Oh, please don't go all that distance away, not when you and I are about to become close friends,' she pleaded.

'It won't be for long, Isobel, for we have to return soon because of the betrothal.'

'Yes, but—'

'We wish to go,' repeated Elizabeth, a little surprised at her vehemence.

Knowing that to say anything more might look a little odd, Isobel fell silent. Her face gave nothing away, but inside she was in turmoil. She had to think of something, for a visit to far-off Norrington Court would not do at all.

The carriage was now halfway along Park Lane, with Hyde Park to the left, and the mansions of Mayfair to the right.

Dawn was lightening the sky more and more, and there were faint lights at the windows as housemaids and other servants went about their early morning tasks.

Aunt Avery's residence, which was almost opposite the Grosvenor Gate entrance to the park, was a handsome four-storied house built of red bricks. It boasted elegant wrought-iron balconies on the upper floors, and the main door was approached by a semi-circular drive through two stone gateways. The coachman maneuvered the carriage in through one of the gateways, and then reined in before the house.

Alexander flung the door open and alighted, turning to extend his hand to Isobel. She descended in a whisper of swansdown, pausing to look back at Elizabeth.

'I will call upon you very soon, Elizabeth,' she said.

'I look forward to it.'

'I trust you do not mean to leave for Lincolnshire within a day or so?'

'Within four days, I should imagine,' Elizabeth replied.

Isobel smiled. 'Good night, and thank you again for bringing me home.' Then she turned to Alexander. 'You cannot possibly know how pleased I am to make your acquaintance, Sir Alexander.'

'I assure you that I am equally as pleased to have met you, Lady Isobel,' he replied, raising her hand to his lips.

She suppressed the telltale shiver of pleasure and then hurried into the house, for her aunt's butler had opened the door in readiness.

Alexander climbed back into the carriage, which drew away the moment the door slammed behind him. As the vehicle swayed out of the other gateway and then began to drive back down Park Lane again, Alexander put his arm around Elizabeth, pulling her closer, and she rested her head on his shoulder.

She closed her eyes for a long, satisfied moment, for it was at times like this that she felt most tranquil and at ease in his company. She would be a fool indeed to put everything in jeopardy simply because of some lingering yearnings from the past. Her days of happiness with James had not lasted very long, but her days of wretchedness at his hands had seemed endless at the time. That was what she must remember now, and she must look forward to her future with Alexander.

The carriage turned west at the foot of Park Lane, then passed through the turnpike gate and out of London along a stone road with the long acres of Hyde Park to the north. The dawn was pale gray now, and the trees in the park were ghostly white with frost. They passed the Jacobean splendor of Kensington Palace, and saw the chimneys of Holland House behind its screen of tall trees, and then they drove through the village of Kensington itself, where Elizabeth looked out a little uneasily at the collection of dilapidated and rather notorious buildings known as the Halfway House. It was a den of thieves and other rogues, and was suspected of being the hiding place of the footpads and highwaymen who had been at work in the neighborhood. But all was quiet now, for even villains must go to their beds, and such low persons did not care for cold or daylight.

Alexander spoke again. 'It was somewhere near here that Tom Crichton believes he saw Marcus.'

'If it was Marcus,' she murmured.

'I hope it was, and I hope too that he chooses soon to seek out his old friends.'

The carriage negotiated the turning from the main road into the narrow lane, which swept down a steep incline to the level meadows that lay between the highway and the distant Thames. The hedgerow was overgrown, with some of the bare-branched trees meeting overhead, and there were very few lights in the houses they passed, but it was only three hundred yards to the gates of Oakgrove House and the twisting gravel drive that led up from the lane to the gracious villa where Elizabeth had lived since returning from Madras.

The villa was very modern indeed, and was not designed to be in the least symmetrical. It was a crenellated, irregular building with all the main reception rooms on the ground floor, each one possessing French doors to the outside so that it was possible to enter and leave the villa from wherever one happened to be at the time. There was an oblong vestibule and staircase hall, a hexagonal drawing room, an oval dining room, a circular library, a square billiard room, and a bow-windowed study that was partly rectangular and partly circular, and upstairs there were bedrooms that echoed these various shapes.

These days it was not only the rage to shun conventional design, but also to go out of one's way to invite nature to invade one's home, and so all the outer walls were carefully trained with climbing and creeping plants, and more plants adorned the balconies upstairs. Flowers and greenery filled every room, and there was a conservatory that was so lush that it resembled a tropical jungle. Oakgrove House was not a large property by society standards, and could not in any way compare with the likes of Devonshire House or Holland House, but Elizabeth had fallen in love with it the moment she saw it, and she had not deemed anywhere else to be even

33

vaguely worthy of inspection.

The carriage drove up the drive and halted, and before alighting Alexander pulled Elizabeth into his arms, holding her close for a long moment. 'I love you with all my heart,' he whispered.

'And I love you,' she replied. It was true, she did love him, but was it the right sort of love?

He sensed that something was wrong. 'What is it, my darling?' he asked, drawing back to look into her eyes.

'What do you mean?'

'Something is troubling you, isn't it? I've felt it for several days now, and sometimes when I look at you I can see that you are preoccupied.'

'There's nothing wrong,' she replied, for how could she possibly tell him what she had been thinking about?

'You would tell me, wouldn't you? I mean, I could not bear it if you had a problem you did not feel able to confide in me.'

She felt suddenly close to tears.

He cupped her face in his hands, brushing his lips over hers. 'You're tired, and I'm keeping you in idle chitter-chatter. I will let you go now, and I promise that we will leave for Lincolnshire as soon as we can, for I think that it will prove a welcome diversion for us both.'

'When will I see you next?'

'Well, there is an exhibition of sporting prints at Ackermann's Repository tomorrow night, or is it tonight now? Anyway, I would rather like to go, for you know how I like sporting prints, but I know that you cannot abide them, and so perhaps we had better agree that I should go alone.'

She smiled. 'Yes, I think we had, for the thought of exam-ining countless likenesses of pugilists, gun dogs, thoroughbreds, and so on, does not exactly fill me with joy.'

'Then let us meet the morning after. Perhaps we could go for a drive in the park?'

'I would like that.'

'Until then, my darling.'

'Until then.'

He kissed her again, and she held him tightly for a moment. Then he alighted, and assisted her from the carriage. As she stepped down to the gravel drive, the door of the house opened, and candlelight flickered as her butler, Wentworth, emerged in his dressing gown with a three-branched candlestick.

'Good morning, Wentworth,' she said, smiling.

'Good morning, madam. Sir. I trust that you enjoyed the ball?'

'We did indeed, Wentworth,' Alexander replied.

The butler held the candlestick carefully to light Elizabeth's way as she stepped into the house. He was a stout man of medium height, with spiky gray hair that was concealed beneath a powdered wig. He wore a plain brown dressing gown over his rather long nightshirt, and there were comfortable slippers on his feet. He shivered in the bitterly cold dawn air, and his breath was clearly visible as he stifled a yawn.

Alexander climbed into the carriage for the last time, and as it drew away once more, Wentworth turned to come into the house, closing the door quietly behind him.

The oblong entrance hall had pristine white walls and floor tiled in green, gray, and white. There was a marble fireplace where the fire had been carefully tended throughout the night, and several elegant green velvet sofas scattered with golden cushions. The doors of several rooms opened off this part of the house, and each one was guarded on either side by a handsome bay tree in an ornate terra-cotta pot. The columns supporting part of the landing on the next floor were twined with climbing plants, and the staircase itself was adorned with pots containing hothouse hyacinths, daffodils, and jonquils. There was a handsome crystal chandelier, but it was unlit, its drops shining faintly in the light from the fire and the butler's candlestick.

Elizabeth went to the fire, held her hands out to the warmth, and gazed thoughtfully into the glowing heart of the flames.

Wentworth waited patiently, but as she remained there, he cleared his throat slightly. 'Madam?'

'Mm?'

'Shall I light you to your room, madam?'

She turned then. 'Light another candle for me, Wentworth, and I will go up in a while. Please tell Violet that she does not need to wait upon me, for I will attend to everything myself.'

'Very well, madam.' He went to a table where various candlesticks were kept in readiness, and when he had lit one of them for her and brought it to the mantelpiece, he bowed again, and then withdrew.

As his footsteps died away, and silence descended over the house, she returned her attention to the fire, her thoughts winging away from the bitter cold of a London winter, to the heat and dust of a burning hot Madras summer. It was the day she had first begun to realize that James was not the man she believed him to be, and the memories were so real in that moment that she could almost smell the camphor-wood furniture in her bedroom, and hear the temple bells in the distance. James had been out all the previous night, and now it was midday, with the sun so high and hot that she had had to retire to her room to lie down. She did not know where he was, and she was anxious. What if something had happened to him? She lay back on the bed, gazing up at the muslin draperies that kept the insects away. So many insects, constantly whining, droning, and buzzing.

Then she heard James approaching the door, his steps uneven with drink. She sat up uneasily, gasping as he flung the door aside and staggered in. His handsome face was distorted with anger, and he carried a glass of cognac which he drained before dashing it to the parquet floor, where it shattered into tiny fragments.

The look on his face terrified her, for it was the face of a stranger. With a cry of fear she scrambled away, but her bed stood against the wall, and she had nowhere to go.

He lurched toward her, pausing to steady himself on the bedpost. His blue eyes were dark with emotion, and his voice was rough with jealous fury. 'You are the talk of Madras, madam. Did you know?'

'Please, James. . .'

'It seems there are few gentlemen here who would not give handsomely for a little time in your arms. How many have you obliged already, Elizabeth?'

'None!' she cried, pressing fearfully back against the wall.

His gaze moved hotly over her naked legs, for she wore only a light silk wrap, which had parted as she scrambled away when first he had entered.

'You're mine, Elizabeth, and mine alone. Don't ever forget it!' His Scottish accent was always slightly more pronounced when he had been drinking, but although she had on many occasions seen him a little merry, she had never seen him as evil with liquor as he was now.

'Please leave, James,' she whispered.

'I'll leave when I've taught you a lesson, madam. As I said, you are mine and mine alone, but I have and will continue to sleep with whatever lady takes my fancy. I've betrayed you time and time again, my lovely wife, but you will not ever put horns on me! Do you hear me?'

Her eyes were huge with fear. 'I hear you,' she replied.

'And now for your lesson!' He lunged forward suddenly, catching the hem of her wrap. She screamed, trying desperately to crawl away from him, but he was too strong. The wrap ripped in his hand, exposing more of her nakedness beneath, and then he gripped her leg, his fingers so vicelike that she cried out with pain.

The bed was soft and warm, but he was hard and cruel. There was no trace now of the skillful lover who had shown her the way to ecstasy; instead he was concerned only with the instant gratification of his own savage desire. He bruised her as he forced himself upon her, and she could taste the cognac on his mouth as he kissed her.

In those dreadful moments she knew more pain and humiliation than she had ever known before, and when he left her battered and scratched, she had whimpered as she curled up wretchedly on the bed.

When next she had seen him he had been sober, but he had remembered what he had done. She knew that he was ashamed of having treated her so vilely, but he told himself that she had been at fault, not he. He did not hurt her again, however, at least, not physically. Mentally he hurt her time and time again, for his infidelities were legion. In the end they cost him his life, for at last he seduced a wife whose husband was a dangerous man to cross. A duel ensued, and James French paid the price of his infamy.

The fire shifted in the hearth, and Elizabeth's thoughts returned to the present. Taking a deep breath, she picked up the lighted candlestick from the mantelpiece, and turned to cross the hall toward the staircase. She could smell the sweetness of the spring flowers as she went up to the next floor, and she blinked back the tears that shimmered on her lashes. Until that dreadful day in Madras she had loved James French with all her heart; he had destroyed her love and her trust, and he had done so in the cruelest possible way.

CHAPTER 4

IT WAS MIDDAY, and Elizabeth slept on in her canopied bed at Oakgrove House. The room was warm, and in virtual darkness, for her maid, Violet, had left the shutters closed and the heavy blue velvet curtains drawn.

The bedroom, which was directly above the drawing-room, was the same size and hexagonal shape. Its walls were hung with blue floral silk, and it had tall windows that on one side opened on to a balcony overlooking the drive, and on the other led to a large balustraded terrace built on the roof of the conservatory. There were ornamental ferns in polished brass bowls, and more hyacinths and daffodils to fill the air with spring fragrance.

Through a doorway there was an adjoining dressing room, furnished in the same way, and lined with mirror-doored wardrobes filled to capacity with an enviable collection of fashionable clothes.

Outside it was still icily cold, and snowflakes were again floating idly on the still air, but they were so few that they could easily have been counted. Sound traveled a long way in such weather, so that the clatter of hooves and wheels carried from the highway across the meadows, but Elizabeth didn't stir until something startled the jackdaws in the elm trees in the lane and they rose noisily from the branches, filling the air with their cries.

Her eyes fluttered and opened, and she stretched lazily between the warm bedclothes. She glanced toward the mantelpiece, and saw the face of the little gilded clock in a chink of light that somehow pierced the shutters and curtains. It was noon!

She sat up, pushing her tangled dark-blonde hair back from her face, then she flung the bedclothes aside and got up, taking her frilled pink woolen wrap from the foot of the bed and slipping quickly into it. She went to one of windows overlooking the drive, drew the curtains back, and then folded the shutters aside. The cold gray light of winter fell across her as she gazed out.

A stagecoach was driving along the highway now, and she could hear its horn wavering out as it approached the turn-pike gate in Kensington village. She could just see the chimneys of Holland House, and in the distance the silhouette of London itself, rising in the winter haze of smoke and freezing air.

The stagecoach horn sounded again as the vehicle passed the entrance to the lane. She remembered what Alexander had said the previous night. Had Tom Crichton seen the mysterious long-lost Marcus Sheridan? Or had it simply been a stranger who resembled him? After all, hadn't she herself seen a golden-haired gentleman in Hanover Square who had reminded her of James?

She was about to turn from the window to ring for Violet, when she heard a carriage in the lane. She could tell by the coachman's briefly shouted command that he was slowing the team to turn into the drive. Someone was calling upon her?

Hesitating by the window, she watched as the horses strained to draw her Aunt Avery's heavy town vehicle up the slope toward Oakgrove House. Why on earth was her aunt calling this morning when they had only seen each other at the ball the night before?

The carriage drew up at the house and Wentworth emerged, going to lower the iron rung and open the door to assist the elderly lady. Maria, Lady Avery, was a diminutive person with a delicately boned face and salt-and-pepper hair that she chose to powder, as had been the fashion in her youth. She wore a dark blue woolen pelisse trimmed with black fur at the collar, cuffs, and hem, and her hands were plunged into a black velvet muff. Her hair was dressed up neatly beneath a black beaver hat adorned with little white plumes, and there were neat black ankle boots on her tiny feet.

After helping her to alight, Wentworth then turned to the carriage again, and Elizabeth realized that her aunt had not called alone, but had brought Isobel with her. Isobel was exquisite in a very modish primrose-yellow jaconet gown that was far from sensible for traveling in such low temperatures, and over it just a rich brown figured velvet spencer. Her chestnut hair was pinned up beneath a primrose silk jockey bonnet from which a brown gauze sca trailed almost to her hem at the back. Elizabeth saw with a start that she had been crying; her face was pale and her eyes tearstained, and she looked as if she had had very little sleep. What was wrong?

As they were shown into the house, Elizabeth turned to

ring quickly for Violet, but as she did so she heard the maid's discreet tap at the door.

'Yes, come in, Violet.'

The maid entered. 'Begging your pardon, madam, but Mr Wentworth saw Lady Avery's carriage coming up the drive and sent me to warn you that she was calling.'

'I know, Violet, she's with my cousin, Lady Isobel.'

'Mr Wentworth will show them into the drawing room and serve them some tea, madam.'

'I will dress as quickly as possible. The lilac muslin, I think, and the gray-and-white cashmere shawl.'

'Madam.' Violet bobbed a curtsy, then hurried through into the dressing room. In spite of her very English name, Violet Dobson, she had a Spanish mother, and it was from her that she took her looks. She had very dark eyes, coal-black hair, an olive complexion, and her figure was thin and neat in a cream woolen gown and crisply starched apron, with a frilled white mobcap on her head.

Elizabeth followed her into the dressing room, drawing the curtains and folding the shutters back herself, before sitting at the dressing table and taking up her hairbrush to do what she could with her tousled curls.

Ten minutes later she was dressed and ready to go downstairs. She inspected her reflection briefly in the cheval glass, turning first one way and then the other to be sure her gown was hanging properly. She was particularly fond of the lilac muslin with its square, pearl-edged neckline and high waistline with the pretty oval mother-of-pearl buckle. Violet had swiftly combed her hair into a creditable knot, leaving a frame of little curls around her face, and now the maid brought the gray-and-white cashmere shawl.

Elizabeth hurried through the house, pausing at the foot of the staircase because the drawing room door stood slightly ajar, and she could see into the room beyond. It was a light, airy chamber, with windows facing toward the front of the house, and glazed doors that opened into the conservatory, and it was hexagonal, like her bedroom directly above. The windows were elaborately draped with rich golden brocade, and the furniture was upholstered in the same material. On the floor there was a handsome Wilton carpet that had been made especially for the house, and once again there were plants and flowers everywhere, in pots, climbing up trellises on the walls, and in bowls upon the tables. And, of course, there was the adjoining conservatory, where tropical greenery pressed prolifically against the glass.

Aunt Avery and Isobel were seated on a sofa by the fireplace, the tea tray untouched on the little table before them. Isobel was dabbing her eyes with a handkerchief, and her aunt was doing her utmost to comfort her.

'There, there, my dear,' she was saying, 'you really must not upset yourself like this, for I am sure that Elizabeth will not mind at all.'

'But . . . but it's such an imposition, especially when she and I do not know each other all that well. Oh, why did this have to happen?' Fresh tears welled from Isobel's beautiful green eyes, and she hid her face in her hands, her slender shoulders trembling as she wept.

Elizabeth was dismayed. Gathering her skirts, she hurried across the entrance hall and into the drawing room. 'Oh, whatever has happened?' she asked, going to crouch before the sofa and take one of Isobel's shaking hands. She looked anxiously at Aunt Avery, fearing the worst, for Isobel's father had long been in poor health. 'Is it the earl?' she asked quickly.

Her aunt nodded. 'Yes, my dear, but do not leap to conclusions, for he is simply very unwell. It seems he fell down the grand staircase at Southwell Park and broke his leg rather badly. Given his already frail constitution, such a mishap has not assisted at all, especially when the winter weather is so very disagreeable. Your Aunt Southwell has written asking Isobel to return home as quickly as possible.'

'Oh, dear. Oh, Isobel, I'm so very sorry,' said Elizabeth, squeezing her cousin's hand. 'Please do not distress yourself too much, for it may be that he isn't as unwell as is thought.'

'He's *terribly* ill, I know he is.' More tears welled helplessly from Isobel's eyes, and she hid her face in her hands again.

Elizabeth looked at Aunt Avery. 'What exactly did the letter say?'

'To be truthful, my dear, I don't really know. When Isobel received it she was so upset that she let it fall, and it went straight into the fire and was immediately burned to a cinder. All I do know is that Isobel's mother wishes her to go back to Southwell Park without delay.'

'Yes, of course she must. But why have you come to me?'

'Well, that is the crux of it, my dear. You see, I am far too old to embark upon such a journey in the middle of winter, and as you know, it is notoriously difficult to engage chaperones of the necessary quality to accompany young unattached ladies. Isobel informs me that you and Sir Alexander are soon to leave for a visit to Norrington Court. Is that correct?'

'Yes, it is.' Elizabeth began to see what was coming.

'It would only be a diversion of a day or so for you to take Isobel home, my dear. As I recall, your route into Lincolnshire doesn't diverge from her route to Nottingham until you reach Colsterworth. Is that not so?'

'Yes.'

'Would it be a great deal to ask, my dear? Would you and dear Sir Alexander escort Isobel home to see her sick father? It would mean a great deal to me, Elizabeth, and I would be eternally grateful.'

It wouldn't have been possible to refuse, even if Elizabeth had wanted to, for at times like this one's family rallied round. 'Of course it isn't a great deal to ask, Aunt Avery,' she replied promptly. 'Isobel is very welcome indeed to join us on the journey, and we will gladly take her all the way to Southwell Park.'

Isobel gave a cry of relief, and flung her arms around Elizabeth's neck. 'Oh, thank you! Thank you! You'll never know how grateful I am!'

'Isobel, how could you possibly have thought I would refuse? I am your cousin, and I wouldn't dream of not helping at such a time.'

'You make me so ashamed of myself. When I think of how odious I used to be, barely speaking to you, and—'

'Don't think any more about it,' Elizabeth interrupted gently, then she smiled at her. 'We must not waste Wentworth's tray of tea, for I am sure that a cup will restore you a little.' She got up, and began to pour the tea into the dainty white-and-gold porcelain cups.

When they were all seated comfortably, Isobel sipped her tea for a moment, and then smiled a little wanly at Elizabeth. 'I will try not to intrude during the journey, Elizabeth, for I am sure that if the truth be known you were looking forward to being alone with Sir Alexander.'

'You will not be intruding, I promise you.'

'If I were in your place, I would regard it as an intrusion,' Isobel declared.

Elizabeth smiled. 'You would?'

'Oh, yes, for if I had snapped up a gentleman as handsome and charming as Sir Alexander, I would not want any other woman anywhere near him.'

'Indeed? He would be flattered to know it,' Elizabeth replied, smiling again.

Isobel lowered her glance to her cup and said nothing more.

Aunt Avery cleared her throat. 'Elizabeth my dear, I am afraid that I have some more rather unfortunate news to tell you; it concerns your old headmistress, Mrs Bateson.'

'Unfortunate news?'

'Yes. I happened to be examining a new consignment of lace at Messrs Clark & Debenham in Wigmore Street.... Have you been there yet, Elizabeth? It's a very new haberdashery, but I vow that it will soon be *the* place to go, for it has the most wonderful variety of lace. Now, where was I?'

'You were about to tell me something about Mrs Bateson.'

'Ah, yes. While I was examining the lace, I was approached by Lady Hargreave-Winterton. Her name will of course be known to you because her daughter, Aurora, was a friend of yours at the seminary. Do you remember Aurora?'

'Yes, of course.'

'Well, it seems that Mr Bateson died about six months ago, leaving such mountainous debts that his unfortunate widow had no option but to sell the academy in order to meet them. She is now reduced to living in a very modest dwelling in Knightsbridge, and has been brought so low by everything that she is a shadow of her former self.'

'I will make a point of calling upon her before we leave for the north. Did you say she now lives in Knightsbridge?'

'Yes, and I believe you will know the very house. Call to mind the bridge over the Westbourne stream and a little double-fronted property on the left as one travels toward London. I believe it has two of those dreadful monkey puzzle trees by the gate. Do you know the house I mean?'

'Yes, I know it. Mrs Bateson lives *there*?' Elizabeth was appalled, for after the grandeur of Hans Place, such a small house was a definite change for the worse.

'It's very sad,' Aunt Avery went on. 'Mrs Bateson and I are acquainted, as you know, and it is my intention that Isobel and I should call briefly upon her on our way home to Park Lane. Perhaps I could tell her that you will call soon, for I know that she particularly likes to see her old pupils again.'

'Yes, please tell her.'

'Do you have a specific time in mind? Tomorrow, perhaps?'

'Yes – er, no. I think I will call upon her this evening, for I am not seeing Alexander.'

'Not seeing him?'

'No, he is taking himself off to Ackermann's to view their exhibition of sporting prints, and I have declined to accompany him, so I can quite easily call upon Mrs Bateson this evening at about seven.'

Aunt Avery wasn't happy. 'My dear, don't you think it a little unwise to go out alone in the dark? I have heard such dreadful tales of footpads and highwaymen in these parts, that I would much prefer you to remain indoors.'

'I admit that we have had some trouble here recently, but the watch patrols more frequently now, and since then we haven't been bothered at all. Besides, if Alexander and I are to travel to Norrington Court soon, there is much to do, and so I would prefer to visit Mrs Bateson as quickly as possible, and leave myself the remaining few days to prepare at leisure, especially as Alexander has promised to take me driving in Hyde Park tomorrow morning.'

'Oh, very well, if you insist, my dear. But take every precaution, won't you?'

'Of course.'

Isobel hadn't said anything for some time now, and her tears had subsided. Her green eyes were thoughtful as she sipped her tea, and a faint smile played upon her lips.

Aunt Avery glanced at the clock on the mantelpiece. 'Goodness, is that the time? These winter afternoons are so very short, that I fear it may be dark before we reach home, for I simply must call upon poor Mrs Bateson on the way. Come, Isobel, we cannot delay.'

'Yes, Aunt Avery,' replied Isobel meekly, replacing her cup and saucer on the tray, and getting up obediently.

Aunt Avery rose to her feet, and turned to Elizabeth. 'Thank you for being so very understanding of poor Isobel's predicament, my dear.'

'Not at all.'

'Just send word to Park Lane when your arrangements are made, and Isobel will fall in with whatever plans you decide upon.'

'Very well.'

Elizabeth accompanied them both out into the entrance hall, where Wentworth was waiting to open the door. Aunt Avery shivered as she stepped reluctantly outside into the cold. 'Oh, dear me, what a dreadful winter this has been so far, and it promises to be much, much worse, from all accounts. I do pray that it holds off long enough for you to accomplish your journey in full, my dear,' she said to Elizabeth.

'I'm sure it will,' Elizabeth murmured, kissing her cheek, and then kissing Isobel.

She watched as they hurried out to the waiting carriage, and as it drove away she went back inside.

Isobel sat back against the rich lavender-scented velvet upholstery, gazing back toward the villa. 'Aunt Avery,' she said after a moment, 'do you think it would be possible for me to visit the exhibition at Ackermann's this evening? I could take my maid, and if the carriage conveys me door-to-door, I cannot possibly come to any harm.'

'Visit Ackermann's on your own? Oh, my dear, I don't know . . .'

'Sir Alexander will be there, and besides, it is rather important.'

'What can possibly be important about visiting an exhibition of sporting prints?' inquired Aunt Avery.

'Well, my father loves such prints, and I thought it would be nice to take him a new one as a present.' Isobel's green eyes were all wide innocence.

Her aunt relented immediately. 'Oh, my dear, what a thoughtful daughter you are, to be sure. Of course you can go.'

'Thank you, Aunt Avery.' Isobel smiled to herself as she gazed out of the carriage window. Things were going excellently. First she had engineered her way into accompanying Elizabeth and Alexander on their journey, and now she would be able to see Alexander at the exhibition when Elizabeth was otherwise engaged with her old headmistress.

She leaned her head back against the carriage seat, humming the tune from *L'Échange*. How fortunate it was that she had received the letter from her mother. Oh, she hadn't fibbed entirely about her father's mishap, she had merely embroidered upon it. Her mother hadn't begged her to return home, but had reassured her that her father would soon recover. Aunt Avery and Elizabeth did not know that, however, and when they all reached Southwell Park, she, Isobel, would simply pretend to have misunderstood the letter.

And who knew what might have transpired by then? She meant to make full use of every moment she got, and if Alexander had not succumbed to her wiles, it would not be for want of trying on her part.

CHAPTER 5

AS EVENING APPROACHED, Elizabeth adjourned to her room to prepare for the promised call upon her old headmistress. Violet was to accompany her, and had already changed into her best green woolen gown and had placed her own mantle as well as her mistress's fur-lined cloak over a chair by the fire to warm for the short journey to Knightsbridge.

Elizabeth chose to wear a simple dusty-pink fustian gown that was both warm and comfortable, and her only jewelry was the pair of gold earrings given to her by her parents. Her hair was combed into a Grecian knot, and over it she wore a wide-brimmed Gypsy hat that was tied on with a wide pink satin ribbon that passed right over the crown and brim and was fixed with a flouncy bow beneath her chin.

The clock on the bedroom mantelpiece struck half-past six as mistress and maid left to go down to the entrance hall, where Wentworth was ready to escort them out to the waiting carriage. It was very dark outside, and the raw cold had not relented at all. The breath of the horses stood out in frozen clouds, and a thin mist obscured the lane at the end of the drive.

The light from the entrance hall shone out palely as the butler assisted Elizabeth into the vehicle, and then Violet. He closed the door upon them, and raised the iron rung, before turning to the coachman, a sturdy, ruddy-faced young man by the name of Frederick.

'Remember now, Frederick, you are to keep a sharp eye open for rogues, and if you see anything suspicious, give the horses full rein. Is that clear?'

'Yes, Mr Wentworth.' Frederick touched his hat. He was dressed in a large coat with four capes over the shoulders, and there was a sheepskin rug tucked over his knees. He wore two pairs of gloves and heavy top boots, but still the cold had crept through to his bones, and this before they had even left the house.

'Drive on then, but do remember to take every care,' Wentworth instructed.

'Sir.'

Touching his hat again, Frederick tooled the team into action, setting them slowly down the curving drive toward the lane. The carriage lamps swung through the thin mist, picking out the silhouettes of trees and shrubs, and then the gateposts came into view, stark and white against the night. Frederick eased the fresh horses out into the narrow lane, and immediately decided not to take any chances at all. Cracking the whip, he flung the team forward, bringing them up to a brisk pace. The carriage swayed alarmingly, and inside Elizabeth and Violet held on tightly to the straps. The speed of the vehicle would have deterred footpads, and would probably have discouraged a mounted highwayman as well, for the lane was very confined, and to stand in the way would have been tantamount to lunacy.

As the carriage drove swiftly up the incline toward the highway, and then successfully drew out to mingle with the other traffic, Elizabeth and Violet sat back with relief.

Frederick now tooled the horses along at a gentle trot, passing Kensington village and the Halfway House, then driving on toward Knightsbridge, and the little house with the monkey puzzle trees.

Elizabeth wondered if Alexander was already viewing the sporting prints at Ackermann's. He would spend hours examining them all, for such things were a particular passion with him, and his house in Cavendish Square boasted one of London's finest collections. She hoped he did not mind that she had agreed to take Isobel with them. She had written to him explaining the moment her aunt and cousin had gone, but there had been no reply. Surely he would not object? No, he wouldn't do that, for he would understand.

She sighed, staring out at the darkness. She wished that she didn't feel so oddly unsettled. Everything had been going so well, she hadn't had a doubt in the world, but then she had for some reason decided to stop to look at the house in Hanover Square. If she hadn't done that, and if she hadn't seen the man who had so briefly conjured James into life again, then all would have remained well. But she *had* gone to Hanover Square, and she *had* seen the golden-haired gentleman, and now everything felt very different.

Frederick slowed the carriage, turning the horses skillfully in between the monkey puzzle trees guarding the entrance of Mrs Bateson's new home. As he drew the vehicle to a standstill and climbed down to open the door for Elizabeth and Violet to alight, the clock on a nearby church struck seven o'clock precisely.

Across London, in the heart of the city, another lady and her maid were alighting from their carriage outside numbers 96–101 The Strand, the impressive premises occupied by Ackermann's Repository of Fine Art.

Isobel paused on the pavement to adjust the folds of the delicate buttermilk silk gown she wore beneath a geranium velvet three-quarter-length pelisse. Her chestnut hair was teased into soft curls around her forehead, and on her head there was a geranium velvet turban draped with thin golden chains. She carried a white swansdown muff, and there was a glittering diamond brooch pinned to her left shoulder. Her green eyes glittered with anticipation as she nodded at her maid, and they both entered the building.

Ackermann's was renowned for the quality and variety of its prints, and was a suitably grand establishment with a superior facade facing the street. A highly polished nameplate stretched across the building above the handsome ground floor windows, and the pedimented entrance boasted a large brightly painted coat-of-arms supported by heraldic beasts. Tonight's exhibition had been extensively advertised in all the best newspapers, and as a consequence a great many fine carriages had converged upon The Strand. The entire building was brightly lit, and as Isobel and her maid stepped inside the drone of conversation seemed to reverberate all around. It was a mostly male gathering, but with a sufficient sprinkling of ladies to make the occasion suitable.

In daylight Ackermann's was well lit by its many tall windows, and the top floor had a glass lantern roof that admirably showed off any items on display there, but now that darkness had fallen, everything was illuminated by chandeliers. The ground floor counters were covered with green cloths and were presided over by young men assistants wearing brown coats and beige breeches. Portfolios and prints were placed on stands, there was a corner where a huge selection of frames could be examined, and the walls were covered from floor to ceiling with prints of every size and description, from small portraits of great pugilists to grand vistas of Newmarket racecourse.

Business was very brisk, so that it was some time before Isobel was able to attract the attention of one of the assistants, and request him to find Sir Alexander Norrington. A small page was dispatched to search every room, and she waited impatiently by the counter, half-fearing that all would come to nothing because Alexander had decided not to come here tonight.

She tried to look relaxed and unconcerned, idly leafing through a sheaf of little engravings of gun dogs, and at last the page returned to tell her that he had found Alexander on the crowded third floor. He conducted her up the staircase at the rear of the building, and her maid kept very close indeed behind her, for fear of losing her in the crush. The page led them to a room at the very back, where Alexander was engrossed in a comprehensive and enticing display of fox-hunting scenes. Isobel gave the page a coin for his pains, and then stood in the doorway, observing Alexander for a moment before he realized she was there.

The room was not as crowded as most of the others, with only about eight other gentlemen and two ladies, and no one paid much attention to her as she stood there feasting her gaze upon the man who had so unknowingly captured her heart.

He wore a charcoal-gray coat with brass buttons, tight cream corduroy breeches, and black top boots, and there was a very full neckcloth at his throat. His hat and gloves rested on a table beside him, and he stood in a pensive pose with one hand to his chin as he surveyed the wall of prints. His brows were slightly drawn together as he pondered which prints to purchase, but to Isobel it seemed that he was beset by some nameless adversity. His pallor seemed more pronounced, and the intensity of his concentration suggested a brooding, stifled passion. He was more her Childe Harold than ever, and she was immediately conscious of a quickening of her pulse and a tightening of her heart. She must win him, she must! Nothing else would do but that he became hers.

Taking a deep breath, she walked into the room after gesturing to her maid to remain outside. Alexander heard her light steps approaching, and turned with quick surprise. 'Lady Isobel? Is it you who seeks me?'

'Yes, Sir Alexander.'

'Forgive me, I had no idea that it was a lady, or I would never have allowed you to come to me.' He smiled, raising her hand to his lips.

She suppressed a shiver of pleasure. Oh, how she adored him. He was everything she could ever desire. . . .

'How may I be of assistance?' he asked.

'I realize that I have taken yet another liberty by seeking you out like this, Sir Alexander, but I require your assistance.'

'I am at your disposal.'

'Well, as Elizabeth will have told you by now, my father has been taken suddenly worse, and—'

'Elizabeth has told me nothing, Lady Isobel, for I have not seen her today. I know that your father has been unwell for a long time now, and if there has been a deterioration I am truly very sorry to hear of it.'

'I am afraid that my father fell down the staircase at Southwell Park, Sir Alexander, and my mother fears greatly for him, as his condition has been severely aggravated by the accident. That is why I must go there as quickly as possible.' Isobel looked quizzically at him. 'If you have not seen Elizabeth, surely she has sent word to you about it?'

'Possibly she has, but I have not been at home today. I breakfasted with Tom Crichton at my club, and then he and I spent most of the rest of the day together. We're endeavoring to find an old friend, but I am afraid we were not successful. I digress, however. You were speaking of your father, and having to go to him.'

'I thought Elizabeth would inform you, Sir Alexander, because she has very kindly agreed that I can travel north with you both, and that you will escort me all the way to Southwell Park so that I may be with my father.'

'I see. Lady Isobel, do I take it that you fear I may object?'

'It is an imposition, sir, and you would be within your rights to object.'

'I would most certainly not be within my rights, for your need is great at such a distressing time. I am truly sorry that you will be accompanying us for such a sad reason, but I am delighted that you will be with us.'

'You are?'

'How could I not be?' He smiled.

She felt quite weak with emotion. Oh, to be free to fling her arms around him and kiss him on the lips. 'You . . . you are very kind, Sir Alexander.'

'I merely wish to do all I can to assist, Lady Isobel.'

'Of course. I – I was hoping that you would help me choose a print to take to my father. Elizabeth says that you know a great deal about such things, but I am afraid that I know very little. My father is very interested in gun dogs.'

'Gun dogs? Well, there is a vast selection of suitable prints to choose from. Come, I will be honored to help you choose something.' He took her hand and drew it gently over his sleeve.

She smiled up into his hazel eyes. 'I envy my cousin Elizabeth, Sir Alexander, for in you she has surely found the most perfect of gentlemen.'

'You flatter me, I think.'

'No, I do not, for you are everything I trust I will one day find for myself.'

'Such one-sided praise will make me swollen-headed, so perhaps I should redress the balance by telling you that I think you look enchanting tonight.'

'Thank you, Sir Alexander,' she breathed, her eyes shining as she allowed him to escort her from the room. She intended to spend several hours with him if possible, and she intended to flatter and admire all she could, without being too obvious. He was going to feel good in her company, better than he felt with Elizabeth, for that was the key.

It was something Aunt Avery had said that had told her how to proceed in her stratagem to win him. 'Make a man feel good when he is with you, my dear, make him feel that he is the only fine fellow in the world, and he will soon be eating out of your hand. Make him feel even slightly uncomfortable, and his glance will stray.'

Elizabeth did not stay long at Mrs Bateson's, for the old lady was very frail and found conversation tiring. It was sad to see her former headmistress brought so low by circumstance, and like several other former pupils who had called before her, Elizabeth saw to it that a sum of money was left to provide for Mrs Bateson's comfort. Promising to call again soon, Elizabeth then left with Violet.

Frederick drove the team out between the monkey puzzle trees, and then back along the highway toward Kensington. Isolated snowflakes swirled in the air again as the lane came in sight ahead, and he slowed the team to a walk to negotiate the sharp turn into the incline that led down to the meadow-land below. The horses balked a little, and Frederick had to gather them. The carriage turned into the lane and was just out of sight from the highway when the shadows emerged from the hedgerow. Dark silent figures grabbed at the startled horses' bridles, and several more leaped quietly on to the carriage itself, scrambling over the top toward Frederick, who at first tried to fling the horses forward, but then took up the whip to try to beat off the attackers. One of the figures on the carriage behind him struck him a blow to the back of the head, and with a grunt he lost consciousness, tumbling down from the carriage to fall heavily to the ground.

Elizabeth and Violet pressed fearfully together inside the carriage, for there was no mistaking what was happening. The vehicle's sudden halt, the frightened horses, and the few swift cracks of the whip had told them all they needed to know.

Violet screamed as the carriage door was suddenly flung open, and a man with a swarthy, unshaven face peered in, his features lit faintly by the light from the carriage lamps.

'Well, if it ain't a pretty lady and 'er maid,' he growled,

grinning a little as they tried to keep as far away from him as possible. He gave them both a parody of a bow, as if he was quite the gallant. 'Step down, if you please, my lovelies,' he invited.

They remained motionless, too frightened to do anything.

His smile was extinguished. 'Do as I say!' he snapped, reaching in to seize Elizabeth's wrist and drag her out.

She resisted, struggling with all her might, but he was far too strong and suddenly she found herself falling from the carriage into the lane, where she lay winded for a moment, only inches away from Frederick's motionless body.

Her eyes widened as she saw the coachman. 'Frederick?'

'There ain't nothin' wrong wiv 'im,' said the man who had dragged her out. Then he turned to Violet, but the maid scrambled out unaided, afraid of angering him.

Elizabeth rose shakily to her feet, backing away until she was against the carriage. 'I haven't any money,' she said. It was true, for what money she'd brought out tonight had been left at Mrs Bateson's.

He grinned. His teeth were black and rotten, and his clothes stank of the stable. 'No money, eh? Well, we'll see about that.' He snapped his fingers toward her reticule, and she handed it over without argument.

He opened it and shook the contents over the ground. Out fell her vial of lavender water, her silver comb, her handker-chief, and the few pennies that were left. He bent to snatch up the vial and the comb, as well as the pennies, but he left the reticule and the handkerchief lying there. Then he looked at her again. 'Come on, now, my dear, I'm sure you've got sommat else for us, ain't you?'

'No,' she whispered.

His glance moved to her earrings. 'They'll do nicely,' he said, holding out his hand.

'Please don't take them, for they were given to me by my parents!'

'Oh, please don't take them,' he mimicked, putting on a silly high voice. His companions enjoyed the joke. His smile faded again. 'Give 'em up, sweetheart, before I take 'em. I won't be gentle, I promise you.'

Close to tears, she removed the precious earrings and dropped them into his outstretched hand. 'That's all the jewelry I have,' she said, holding his gaze.

He gave her another menacing grin. 'P'raps a little kiss?' he breathed, coming closer.

Revulsion and terror washed icily through her, and her desperate glance flew toward the highway, so near and yet so very far away. Here in the lane everything was in shadow, but up there, only yards away, carriages and other vehicles were passing freely to-and-fro. Suddenly she saw a horseman, a gentleman mounted on a spirited coal-black thoroughbred, and in an instant she screamed at the top of her lungs.

'Footpads! Quickly! Help! Help!'

The gentleman reined in, looking down into the lane. Evidently he could make something out, for he reached inside his greatcoat pocket and drew out a pistol, the barrel of which glinted in the lamplight from a swiftly passing gig.

The footpads had frozen the moment she screamed, and then the ringleader pocketed the earrings. 'Scatter, my laddoes!' he shouted, and as one they melted away into the shadows.

Elizabeth stepped tentatively forward, trying to see exactly where the ringleader went. She saw him vault lightly over a gate into one of the meadows and then run away in the direction of Kensington with several of his accomplices. Halfway House – he was going to take refuge in Halfway House!

The gentleman had by now urged his horse down into the lane, and he reined in beside her. 'Are you all right?'

She tore her eyes away from the meadow, and stared up with a shock into the handsome face of the man she had seen emerging from the house in Hanover Square. She recognized him immediately, for he was so very distinctive with his bright golden hair and aristocratically fine features. His eyes were very quick and blue in the light from the carriage lamps.

'Are you all right?' he asked again, reaching down to put a gloved hand to her chin.

'Yes,' she whispered. 'You came in time.'

Frederick was beginning to come around, and Violet knelt anxiously beside him. The gentleman looked at Elizabeth again. 'Did they take anything?'

'My earrings were the only thing of value.' A lump rose in her throat, and tears filled her eyes as she thought of the earrings that meant so much to her.

His hand still cupped her chin. 'They were valuable?'

'I treasured them,' she whispered.

'Then I will do what I can to retrieve them. Did you see which way the footpads went?'

She pointed toward the gate. 'I think they were going to Halfway House.'

'Most probably. You stay here, and I will return as quickly as I can.' Gathering the reins of his horse, he rode toward the gate, pausing only long enough to bend down and swing it open before urging his mount through into the dark meadow beyond.

She stared after him, still shaken to have found herself face to face with the man she had taken so briefly for her late husband.

Silence returned to the lane. The clatter of traffic on the highway seemed muffled, and when one of the carriage horses shook its head suddenly, the jingle of the harness sounded unnaturally loud and almost jarring. Frederick was sitting up now, but was too dazed to do a great deal, and Violet still knelt anxiously beside him.

Elizabeth could hear her own heartbeats, and she gave a frightened gasp as a twig snapped somewhere nearby. Had one of the footpads returned? The others heard the sound as well, and Violet scrambled fearfully to her feet, staring in the direction from which it had come. There was another snap, and Elizabeth suddenly gathered her skirts, hurrying to the others.

'We cannot stay here. Frederick, do you think you can climb into the carriage?'

'*Into* it, madam?'

'Yes. Violet and I can lead the horses back to the house.'

'I'll try, madam . . .'

They helped him carefully to his feet, both still glancing nervously over their shoulders, half-expecting to see the footpads coming toward them again.

Frederick clambered into the carriage as best he could, and they closed the door upon him before hastening to the horses, and beginning to lead them along the lane. They hurried as swiftly as possible, urging the nervous team to do their bidding, and at last they saw the white posts of the house ahead.

They managed to persuade the horses to negotiate the turn

into the drive, and soon the welcome lights of Oakgrove House swung into view. There was no one behind them as they led the team toward the door.

The footpads thought themselves safe, and now strolled quite openly across the highway toward Halfway House. There were still carriages passing to-and-fro, and they didn't hear the single horseman riding swiftly up behind them. The first they knew was when they reached the verge on the other side of the road, and a cool voice commanded them to halt or know the consequences.

They froze in a pool of light from a lantern on the corner of a building, and as they slowly turned they saw the gentleman on his thoroughbred, his pistol leveled at them. He had detected them in the meadow, and had overheard enough of their unguarded conversation to know that they were the ones who had robbed the carriage in the lane. He had had only to wait until they were out in the open, where there were sufficient lights to see them accurately. . . .

The ringleader spread his hands in a gesture of innocence. 'What d'you want wiv us, guv'?'

'The earrings you stole a few minutes ago,' replied the gentleman, slowly cocking his pistol. The sound carried ominously to their ears.

'Earrings, guv'?' said the ringleader, shifting his position uncomfortably.

'Don't play the innocent with me, for I've heard enough of your conversation to know you did it. Hand them over.'

The footpad's eyes darkened with anger, but he didn't want to risk the squeezing of any trigger. 'We meant no 'arm, guv',' he said, taking the earrings from his pocket and holding them out in the palm of his hand.

'Bring them to me,' commanded the gentleman, swinging the pistol toward the man's heart. 'And no tricks, my friends, or it will be the worse for you.'

'No tricks, I promise, guv',' murmured the man, walking slowly toward him, the earrings still in the palm of his hand.

The gentleman was no fool, and guessed that the man meant to throw them. He took very careful aim with the pistol. 'One swift move now, my friend, and I'll put an immediate end to you. Move very slowly indeed if you know what's good for you.'

A nerve flickered at the man's temple, and he thought better of trying anything. 'You've got the better of me, guv'. I won't do nothin', I swear it.'

'Don't be foolish enough to test me,' breathed the gentleman, reaching down carefully with one hand, while still keeping the pistol trained upon the man's heart.

The man slowly dropped the earrings into the outstretched hand, and then backed away. He reached his companions, and they all hesitated, wondering what would happen next.

The gentleman's swift glance went toward the surrounding buildings. It was a warren of villains, and one shot would bring them all pouring out. He wanted no further trouble, for he had got what he had come for. He pushed the earrings into his pocket, and then backed his horse slowly away, the pistol still cocked. He could hear another carriage approaching, and he waited until it had drawn alongside him, then he sharply turned his horse, kicking his heels and urging it across the highway behind the carriage.

The footpads gave a shout and began to give chase, but

then halted again, for he had vanished into the shadows at the far side of the road, and they knew that he had got away.

With a satisfied laugh, the gentleman rode easily back across the meadow toward the gate into the lane, but as he drew near he could not see the telltale glow of carriage lamps. Reining in by the gateway, he glanced up and down the now deserted lane. Then he saw something small and white lying on the ground, and he dismounted to see what it was.

He picked up a lady's handkerchief, embroidered with flowers and trimmed with lace. Instinctively he raised it to inhale the perfume of lavender, and then he smiled a little. Who was she, his mysterious lady in distress? Well, maybe he would never know now, for she had flown.

Remounting, he urged the horse back up toward the highway, and then continued on his way as if nothing had ever interrupted his journey.

CHAPTER 6

ISOBEL STOOD AT her bedroom window overlooking Hyde
Park. The morning sunlight was cold and clear, and the trees
were still white with frost. A constant stream of carriages
drove in and out of Grosvenor Gate, and there was a caval-
cade of elegant and fashionable riders enjoying the display of
Rotten Row. She was sure she could hear the distant laughter
and shouts of the people skating on the ice-covered
Serpentine.

She glanced back at her reflection in the graceful gilt-
framed cheval glass in the dressing room behind her. She was
dressed in modish walking clothes, an amber woolen pelisse
trimmed with white fur and a matching amber gown that was
embroidered with white rosebuds. Her hair was twisted up
beneath a white fur hat, and on her feet she wore neat little
ankle boots that were laced at the back. A brown velvet reticule was looped over her wrist, and she flexed her slender
fingers a little impatiently in her gloves as she returned her
attention to the scene outside. Her gaze raked the traffic
approaching from the southern end of Park Lane, seeking one
carriage in particular, Alexander's town vehicle, for Elizabeth

had said that they would be driving in the park this morning, and she, Isobel, meant to turn the occasion to her own advantage, just as she had made full use of the Ackermann's exhibition the evening before.

A faint smile played upon her lovely lips as she thought of the previous evening. How good it had been to spend so long alone in his company, and how flatteringly attentive he had been. No one could have been more helpful and thoughtful, going to endless lengths to make sure that the perfect print was chosen for her father. A sliver of guilt touched her for a moment, and she lowered her glance to the windowsill. It was very wrong to pretend that her father was much more ill than he really was, but so strong were her feelings for Alexander that she had not thought twice about employing such a reprehensible device. She was far from proud of herself, but where Alexander was concerned she was prepared to ignore such minor complications as pangs of conscience. Taking a deep breath she looked outside again, determined to proceed with the plan she had embarked upon at the Duke of Devonshire's ball. She was going to win Alexander, and she could still tell herself that there was nothing wrong with such a course because Elizabeth did not really love him as he should be loved.

She began to hum softly to herself, and again the tune she chose was the melody from *L'Échange*. She was going to make the new cotillion come true, and was going to supplant Elizabeth as Alexander's partner.

At that moment Alexander's carriage was approaching the southern corner of Park Lane. The team of beautifully matched grays stepped high, harness jingling, and the gleaming dark green vehicle swayed as its bright yellow wheels rattled over the stones. Inside there was an awkward atmosphere, with both occupants gazing silently out of the windows.

Elizabeth was close to tears, for it was upsetting to have fallen out with Alexander so quickly after the frightening events of the night before. Her hands twisted disconsolately in her peach fur muff, and she bit her lip, determined not to show by so much as a single tear that she was really far from composed. She had awoken that morning in an extremely unsettled mood, filled with reservations about her forth-coming betrothal, and still distressed about the robbery. She felt guilty, too, wondering if her gallant rescuer had returned as he had promised. How ungrateful he must think her.

Opposite her, Alexander was also feeling far from happy. He gave a silent sigh, shifting his position slightly on the seat. He wore a wine-red coat, greenand-white-floral brocade waistcoat, and pale gray breeches, and his tall-crowned hat was tipped back on his dark hair. He rested one arm along the window ledge of the carriage, and his gloved fingers drummed restlessly as he stole a secret glance at Elizabeth.

She looked lovely in a stylish gray velvet pelisse and peach gown. There was peach embroidery on the pelisse, gray embroidery on the gown, and on her head she wore a gray straw bonnet adorned with delicate peach-and-gray gauze scarves that were tied in a huge bow beneath her chin. Soft dark-blond curls edged her face, which looked rather pale and tired; she had not slept well the night before, and prior to that there had been the ball, which had gone on until dawn. He wanted to reach out to her and take her in his arms to comfort her, but words had been exchanged and he was angry. He was also plagued with remorse, for when she had been terrorized while at the mercy of footpads, he had been laughing and enjoying himself with Isobel at Ackermann's. To salve this remorse he had told himself that he could hardly have been expected to know what was happening, indeed he had not known anything until this morning, when Wentworth had informed him. Elizabeth should have sent for him the night before, or at the very least she should have sent word telling him what had happened, but she had not done either. He was very concerned for her, but he was also angry that he had been excluded in her hour of need. It was anger that had bubbled to the surface as soon as they were alone in the carriage.

He closed his eyes for a moment, recalling the conversation. He had begun on an unbecoming note of which he was now ashamed. 'Elizabeth, do you not think it would have been courteous to have let me know about last night?'

'There was nothing you could have done.'

'I could have come to you, or did you perhaps think my comfort was of so little consequence that you could not be bothered with it?'

Her gray eyes had flown reproachfully to his face. 'Oh, Alexander, you know that that isn't so.'

'I don't know any such thing. Why didn't you send for me?'

'Because the whole business was over and done with, and I saw no point in ruining your evening. You'd been looking forward to examining all those prints, and I didn't want to spoil it for you.'

'I would have preferred to have been with you when you

needed me, Elizabeth. Besides, Isobel and I . . .'

'Isobel?' She had looked quickly at him. 'Isobel was with you?'

He had felt unaccountable color rush into his cheeks. 'Er – yes. At least, we did not accompany each other there, rather did she seek me out to help her choose a print to take to her father. We spent some time deliberating, and in the end decided upon a particularly handsome likeness of a Newfoundland retriever. I understand your uncle is particularly fond of gun dogs.'

'I have never known him to display such a decided fondness, but that does not necessarily signify since I have not visited Southwell Park very frequently in recent years. Did you escort Isobel home afterward?'

The color had remained on his cheeks. 'Yes. Actually she expressed a wish to sit with me in my phaeton, and so her carriage followed.'

'You should not have done that, Alexander. My aunt would not be best pleased to learn that Isobel was with you without her chaperone. I take it that she did visit Ackermann's in company with her maid?'

'Yes, of course she did, and the maid could see us all the time. Elizabeth, we did not offend propriety in any way last night, I assure you.'

'I do not for a moment imagine that you did,' she had replied. 'I am just pointing out that it would have been wiser to have insisted that Isobel return in her carriage.'

'And as far as you and I are concerned, it would have been wiser if you had sent for me last night,' he had replied, the words slipping out almost before he knew they were in his head.

Her lips had parted in surprise. 'What do you mean by that?'

'Simply that I no longer know where I am with you, Elizabeth. In recent days you've been withdrawn and almost unapproachable at times. You insist that all is well, but I know it isn't. Are you going to confide in me, or not?'

'There is nothing to confide.' But she had not met his eyes.

He had fallen silent for a moment, not wanting to continue in the same vein, but unable to help himself. 'And what of this mysterious Sir Galahad?'

'Sir Galahad?'

'Your dashing rescuer?'

She flushed a little. 'That is all there is to tell. He came when I called for help, and then he rode off to try to retrieve my earrings. We thought the footpads were returning, and so Violet and I led the carriage back to the house. I do not know who the gentleman was, and I don't even know if he returned to the lane as he promised. I wish now that we had stayed there, for it was hardly courteous to run away as we did.'

'He didn't introduce himself?'

'It wasn't a time for observing politeness, Alexander,' she had replied a little shortly.

'So it seems. Tell me, Elizabeth, why was it acceptable for you to turn to this unknown fellow for assistance, but a little questionable for me to help Isobel choose a print for her father?'

She had stared at him, totally taken aback. 'Alexander, I haven't even remotely suggested that it was not in order for you to assist Isobel.'

'No? It seems to me that you are reading more into the matter than there is to read.'

73

'If that is how it seems to you, then I can only repeat that you are wrong,' she had replied sharply. 'And as to my having turned to a stranger for assistance, perhaps you think it would have been better if I'd remained silent and allowed the footpads to do as they wished? I do not think that they had just robbery in mind, indeed I am sure they did not, and that if it had not been for my so-called Sir Galahad, then I fear to imagine what fate might have befallen Violet and me.'

Contrition had descended over him then. 'Elizabeth, I—'

'Please don't say anything more, Alexander, for I would prefer not to argue further. So far this morning you have done nothing but find fault with me, and now I simply wish to complete this disagreeable drive in silence.'

That was where the matter had been left, and nothing could have been more unsatisfactory. In his heart he knew that the fault had been his, but it was still true that she had been in an odd humor recently. Sometimes he felt that a great chasm separated them, and it was a feeling that was beginning to affect him. He loved her, the Lord knew he loved her, but her withdrawal made it very difficult indeed. . . .

The carriage was approaching Grosvenor Gate, and was forced to slow as it joined the many other vehicles that converged on the same spot in order to take part in the fashionable daily turn around Hyde Park, the 'lungs' of London. Neither Elizabeth nor Alexander glanced toward Aunt Avery's house opposite, nor did they see Isobel's figure in the window. The carriage negotiated the turn through the gate, and Isobel gathered her skirts to hurry down through the house to where her maid was waiting in the vast marble entrance hall. A moment later they emerged into the cold morning air, quickly crossing Park Lane to enter the park.

Meanwhile, the carriage had passed the famous Gloucester Riding School, which lay just inside Grosvenor Gate, and was now driving south with all the other vehicles making the circuit of the park. The thud of hoofs and jingle of harness filled the air, as did the excited yelping of the elegant greyhounds that loped at the heels of their masters' glossy Arabian horses, for it was very much the thing for gentlemen of fashion to keep such horses and hounds simply for the parade in the park. Lacquered carriage panels gleamed in the sunlight, and perfectly matched teams tossed their fine heads as London's *haut ton* took the air.

The park was famous for its avenues of oaks, chestnuts, and elms, and was cool and leafy during the hot summer months, but there were no leaves now, just frosty branches forming a lacework against the cold blue sky. The waters of the Serpentine were now a sheet of ice upon which countless enthusiastic skaters endeavored to show off their skill, or lack of it, and a great crowd had gathered because a rather tipsy young blood was causing havoc by driving his cabriolet over the frozen surface. His whip cracked and the horse picked up its heels in a spirited trot as the light vehicle skimmed over the ice, occasionally slipping from side to side and threatening to overturn.

Elizabeth sat forward, her eyes widening as she watched the breathtakingly reckless display. 'Is he mad?' she gasped, her heart almost stopping as the young gentleman turned his horse sharply to the right, and the cabriolet slid alarmingly to one side.

Alexander had been observing as well, and now he nodded. 'Well, since he happens to be the Honorable Horace Skiffingworth-Smythe, I think one may safely say yes, he is totally mad. I believe that last week he won a wager that he could drive his cabriolet up the steps of St. Paul's Cathedral.' He smiled at her.

She was glad of the olive branch, and returned the smile.

He reached out, putting his gloved hand to her pale cheek. 'Please forgive me, my darling,' he said softly.

'If you will forgive me.'

'With all my heart. I'm sorry I've been behaving poorly this morning, but I was truly alarmed when I heard what had happened to you. I felt guilty for having been enjoying myself at Ackermann's when you were in such danger.'

'I should have sent word to you. I did not mean to hurt your feelings by not doing so, you do know that, don't you?'

'Of course,' he whispered. He sat back then. 'It will do us both good to escape to Lincolnshire for a while, for London can be very tiring.'

'When will we be able to leave?'

'The day after tomorrow if you wish.'

'Of course I wish.' She smiled again.

'But what if Isobel isn't ready to leave then?' he asked suddenly.

'She will have to be ready,' Elizabeth replied firmly.

'I'm sure she will be,' he said after a moment. 'She is really very charming, so charming that I find it hard to believe that you and she are not close.'

'Well, as I said, she appears to have turned over a very new leaf since last she and I met.' Elizabeth grinned a little impishly. 'Do you know, I am quite convinced that Isobel has noted your astonishing likeness to Childe Harold. She probably believes you to be all that is romantic and wonderfully wicked.'

He colored again. 'Plague take Byron and his confounded hero,' he muttered.

'Just think of all the conquests you could be making if it were not for your forthcoming betrothal to me,' she teased.

'I have no doubt that I could embark upon countless such seductions, but even such foolish females would very swiftly realize that Childe Harold and I have very little in common.'

The carriage continued its circuit, and soon approached Grosvenor Gate again. As it did so, Alexander's attention was drawn to a slender figure in eye-catching amber. 'I say, isn't that Isobel?' he said, sitting forward.

Elizabeth followed the direction of his gaze, and saw her cousin walking into the park with her maid. 'Yes, it is,' she replied.

'We must stop.' Alexander picked up his cane, which lay on the seat beside him, and rapped it peremptorily against the roof of the carriage. The coachman immediately began to rein in.

Alexander lowered the window glass in the door. 'Good morning, Lady Isobel,' he called.

Isobel turned, pretending not to have already noticed the approaching carriage. 'Why, Sir Alexander, what an unexpected pleasure it is to see you again.' She halted, smiling up at him.

He opened the door and alighted beside her, taking her little gloved hand and raising it to his lips. 'You look as beautiful as ever, my lady,' he said.

An irresistible tingle of delight shivered through her, and for a moment she couldn't reply, but then she smiled again. 'And you are as gallant, sir,' she murmured, turning reluctantly toward Elizabeth, who had remained in the carriage.

'Good morning, Elizabeth.'

'Good morning, Isobel.'

Alexander suddenly realized that he was still holding Isobel's hand, and he released it quickly. 'Er – I am afraid that while you and I were enjoying Ackermann's, Lady Isobel, Elizabeth was enduring a horrible experience at the hands of a gang of footpads.'

Isobel's eyes widened. 'Oh, no! Oh, poor Elizabeth. Did they steal anything?'

'My gold earrings.' Elizabeth had to look away, for the loss of the earrings cut very deep.

Alexander reached quickly into the carriage to put his hand reassuringly on her arm. 'Maybe you will recover them,' he said gently.

'I do not think that I will,' she replied, still close to tears.

Isobel noted how quick and sincere this concern was, and she resented it. Last night she had had his full attention, and Elizabeth had scarcely even been mentioned, but now it was Elizabeth who was occupying the center of the stage. That wouldn't do at all, no, indeed it would not. . . . Isobel's mind raced as she sought some way of gaining his attention for herself again, while at the same time calling James French to mind once more. Inspiration came from nowhere. She smiled sympathetically at Elizabeth.

'Oh, I'm so very sorry to hear about the earrings, for I know how much they meant to you. James gave them to you, didn't he?'

'No, they were a gift from my parents.'

'Forgive me,' Isobel said quickly, successfully willing some embarrassed color into her cheeks. 'I . . . I thought that James gave them to you when you and he were first . . . when you first fell in love,' she finished, apparently covered with becoming confusion. She cleared her throat a little. 'I – er – I had to come out into the fresh air this morning, for I fear I am not feeling all that well. I awoke with a dreadful headache, and think it must have been due to all that noise at Ackermann's. We were there for such a long time, were we not, Sir Alexander?'

'Yes, we were. I trust you are feeling better now, Lady Isobel?'

'Actually, I feel a little . . . a little . . .' Isobel's eyelids fluttered, and with a sigh she pretended to faint.

Alexander caught her straightaway, his arms firm and safe around her slender figure. 'Lady Isobel?' he cried in alarm.

Elizabeth gasped, and began to alight, but already Isobel was pretending to come around. She was weak and clinging, giving a little moan as she slipped her arms around his neck and hid her face against his collar as if trying not to cry. 'Oh, Sir Alexander, I feel quite dreadful,' she murmured.

'We'll take you home,' he replied gently, and then he nodded at her startled maid. 'Hurry back to the house and warn them what has happened. Tell them we will bring your mistress in the carriage.'

'Yes, sir.' The maid bobbed a curtsy and then fled out through Grosvenor Gate.

Elizabeth stepped quickly down, looking anxiously at Isobel, whose face was still hidden against his collar. 'Isobel? Can you hear me?'

'Mmm?' The reply was a soft sound that conveyed only partial consciousness.

Elizabeth turned to Alexander. 'Can you lift her into the carriage?'

'Yes, of course, for she is as light as a feather,' he replied, sweeping Isobel up into his arms. 'I'm sure this has happened because she is so distressed over her father,' he said as he stepped effortlessly up into the carriage.

Elizabeth remained outside watching. There was a small oval mirror on the wall of the vehicle, just above the seat; it was there so that ladies could always be sure of keeping their coiffure looking perfect. Now it served to afford Elizabeth a glimpse of Isobel's face. Instead of being closed with faintness, the green eyes were open, and very clear and alert. It was only a brief glimpse, but it made Elizabeth's lips part in surprise.

Alexander could not disengage his burden's dainty arms in order to lay her down on the seat, and so he sat down with her still in his arms.

Elizabeth leaned into the carriage, looking curiously at her cousin's now closed eyes. 'Isobel? Can you hear me?' she asked again.

There was no response, not even a weak moan.

Elizabeth stared at her for a long moment and then climbed into the carriage once more. As the door closed behind her, the coachman stirred the team into action for the short drive out of the park and across the busy thoroughfare to Aunt Avery's residence.

As the carriage began to move, Elizabeth glanced out at the other vehicles and riders who were entering and leaving the park. Her gaze was drawn immediately to a tall gentleman mounted on a coal-black thoroughbred. He wore a dark brown coat with shining brass buttons, and a diamond pin sparkled in the folds of his starched neckcloth. His tall-crowned hat was drawn well forward, but still she could see the bright golden hair and piercing blue eyes of her rescuer of the night before. Her breath caught, and she turned swiftly as he urged his horse past without glancing at the carriage.

'Alexander! That's him! That's the gentleman who helped me!' she cried.

Isobel was afraid that even now Alexander's attention might return to Elizabeth, and so she gave a loud moan, clinging even more tightly to him.

He looked anxiously down at her, and Elizabeth tore her eyes away from the intriguing stranger. When next she looked, he was nowhere to be seen among the throng of horsemen entering Rotten Row.

Alexander smiled apologetically. 'Forgive me, I didn't see. Are you sure it was him?'

'Yes, perfectly sure. You see, he's very like—' She broke off abruptly.

'Yes?' Alexander prompted curiously.

'Very like James,' Elizabeth finished reluctantly.

Alexander didn't reply, and Isobel gave a secret smile.

CHAPTER 7

EARLY ON ANOTHER sunny but frosty morning two days later, two fine traveling carriages set off on the Old North Road on the first stage of the one-hundred-and-sixty mile journey to Southwell Park, which lay on the western edge of Sherwood Forest. The first carriage conveyed Alexander, Elizabeth, and Isobel, while the second contained the two ladies' maids and Alexander's man. It was expected that the journey would be accomplished with only two overnight halts, at inns in Huntingdon and Grantham, unless, of course, the weather intervened to slow them down or maybe even stop them altogether. But as the villages on the outskirts of London began to slip away behind them, the skies were settled and clear, without so much as a hint of the snow that had seemed in the offing for so long now.

For the journey Elizabeth had chosen to wear a cheering shade of strawberry-pink. Her high-collared woolen pelisse was trimmed at the throat, cuffs, and hem with soft gray fur, and beneath the warm pelisse her gown was made of cozy creamy-white fustian. Her hair was drawn up beneath a strawberry velvet hat that had a little net veil covering most of her face. A heated brick wrapped in cloth rested beneath her feet, and her hands were thrust deep into a gray velvet muff that was scattered with little pink satin bows. She was in a quiet mood, for she had not slept well since the night of the robbery, but her quietness was barely noticed because of Isobel's apparent determination to be agreeable company.

It seemed that Elizabeth's cousin had made a vow not to be dull, for she positively sparkled with amiability. She gave no outer sign of her anxiety over her father, and she appeared to have recovered completely from the indisposition that had caused her to faint at Grosvenor Gate. The bitterly cold weather did not seem to affect her, for she wore emerald-green silk that was inappropriately flimsy, if exceedingly stylish and fashionable. That particular shade of green was perfect for someone of Isobel's coloring, for it enhanced her eyes and gave a sheen to her chestnut hair.

Alexander made little secret of the fact that he found Isobel very agreeable indeed. He smiled at her little remarks, and twitted her indulgently now and then as he lounged in his seat next to Elizabeth. The astrakhan collar of his greatcoat was turned up, his tall hat was worn at a rakish angle, and he stretched his long legs out as comfortably as he could in the confinement of the carriage. He wore Hessian boots, and their golden tassels swayed to the rhythm of the vehicle as it bowled northward along the broad highway.

Isobel's frivolous chatter faded away into the background as Elizabeth looked out at the wintry scene. Although the sun was now high in the sky, there wasn't sufficient warmth in it to melt the frost. Cattle huddled together in the fields, their breath visible, and the smoke from chimneys rose almost vertically in the still air. It was the sort of January day that was memorable for its clarity and almost cleansing beauty. The coachmen were able to make excellent time in such conditions, for there hadn't been any rain in a long time and so there wasn't any ice to make the going treacherous. It was confidently expected that they would reach the George Inn at Huntingdon just as darkness fell, and thus avoid the danger of traveling after sunset.

Elizabeth's thoughts drifted, as so often they did now. For the thousandth time she recalled her fateful decision to look at the house in Hanover Square. If it had not been for that, and the fact that she had seen the gentleman leaving the house. . . . No, that particular decision had not made any real difference, for she had been destined to see him on two more occasions after that. She wished again that she knew who he was, for he had kindled old memories that seemed to become stronger and more persistent with each day. She longed for the happiness and passion she had once shared with James, but she had to accept that such things would never be so fully shared with Alexander.

She glanced at Alexander as he smilingly humored Isobel. Surely he was everything any sensible woman could ever wish for? And after her eventually abysmal experience with someone like James, it was the height of folly to want to return to such things, but she simply could not help herself.

Midday came and went, and the countryside changed to the flat fenlands of Cambridgeshire, where the teams could come up to a smart canter. Cambridgeshire gave way to Huntingdonshire as the brief afternoon wore on, and when at last the country town appeared ahead, the sunset was a brilliant but oddly cold crimson. As the carriages drove slowly over the ancient stone bridge spanning the wide River Ouse, they had traveled sixty miles since leaving London.

The George was a bustling hostelry, with ostlers hurrying to-and-fro from the many stagecoaches that called there, ticket office bells summoning the passengers, and maids taking trays up and down the wooden staircase that led to the gallery encircling the yard. Horses whinnied and stamped, harness jingled, iron-rimmed wheels echoed on cobbles, grooms and coachmen shouted, and there was the sound of rather boisterous singing coming from the taproom, where a gathering of local farmers had been sampling the inn's hospitality since midday. The smell of food hung in the air, and now that the sun had almost sunk beyond the western horizon, the windows and doorways were all brightly lit, and lanterns cast pools of light over the scene.

The landlord himself hastened out to attend the two newly arrived carriages, for he had very swiftly perceived Alexander's coat-of-arms on the panels, and guessed that the vehicles contained persons of quality accompanied by their servants. Guests of importance were always personally attended, and he barely waited for the vehicles to finally halt before he had stepped up to the first one to lower the rungs and fling open the door. He was a tall, muscular man, with a bald head and rosy face, and he kept a very prosperous house of which he was justifiably proud, a fact that was written large in his smile as he bowed to them.

'Welcome to the George, sir, ladies. Do you and your

servants require refreshment and accommodation for the night?'

'We do,' replied Alexander, alighting first. 'We would like three of your best chambers for ourselves, and the appropriate arrangements for our servants.'

'Certainly, sir.' The landlord snapped his fingers at a waiter who was on his way back empty-handed to the kitchens. 'See that the three rooms at the front are made ready quickly, and that the same number of servants are to be properly fed and housed,' he said brusquely.

'Sir.' The waiter scuttled swiftly away, his; starched apron rustling audibly in spite of the noise all around.

The landlord turned to Alexander again. 'I can promise you every comfort, sir, and I believe that I may safely boast about the quality and variety of my table.'

'I'm glad to hear it,' replied Alexander, extending his hand to assist Elizabeth and Isobel down from the carriage.

'If you will come this way, sir, ladies,' said the landlord, bowing again and then conducting them toward an illuminated doorway.

As the inn's grooms and ostlers hurried forward to attend to the carriages, the servants alighted to take their master and mistresses' overnight valises from the carefully packed luggage at the rear of the vehicles, and then they too went into the inn.

They entered a high-ceilinged passage lined on one side with high-backed settles and rows of hooks for travelers' coats and cloaks, and on the other with a number of tables providing bowls of warm water, soap, and fresh towels. The floor was stone-flagged and uneven, the walls newly whitewashed, and there were several doors, one of them opening into a crowded dining-room. Above the doors there were sets of antlers, and next to the dark staircase at the far end of the passage there was a huge stuffed bear that stood fiercely on its hind legs.

The landlord promised them a private dining room and a roast pork dinner, and then instructed a maid to conduct them up to their rooms. She carried a wax candle to light the way, and they followed her up the staircase. It had been a long day, and the thought of refreshment and then sleep was appealing to everyone.

Elizabeth's room was candlelit and warmed by a roaring fire that had been hastily encouraged by the addition of several tinder-dry logs. It overlooked the street, and contained a large four-poster bed with a faded green tapestry canopy that revealed it to have originally come from a large house. There were some Axminster rugs scattered on the wooden floor, and apart from the bed there was a wardrobe, a table and chair, a washstand, and a screen to exclude the draft from the door. It was all very clean and tidy, and the bed looked comfortable. Elizabeth was hopeful of enjoying a restful night, but first she had to change to go down to dinner.

The overnight valise contained a suitable gown made of sky-blue marguerite, which would be worn tonight and again the following night when they reached Grantham. Violet quickly unpacked it, and shook out the few creases it had acquired during the day. Then Elizabeth washed her face and hands before changing and sitting at the table while the maid attended to her hair, which was soon pinned up into a Grecian knot of some elegance, with little curls framing her forehead. Normally the golden earrings would have been worn with this particular gown, but instead she had to make do with some drop-pearls that were pretty, but which she would not have chosen if she had still had the other earrings. Half an hour later she was ready to go down to the private dining room the landlord had indicated earlier, and Violet was free to go to the kitchens to join her friends.

As Elizabeth entered the private room, she saw immediately that Isobel had again elected to flout common sense in favor of the height of fashion. Instead of wearing a gown made of something warm like marguerite, she chose to wear a lemon muslin that was so sheer and delicate that it would have been far more appropriate at Devonshire House than here in a provincial inn. Her shining chestnut hair was pinned up into an exceedingly elaborate knot that was adorned with a jeweled comb, and the gown's daring decolletage was accentuated by a heart-shaped gold locket that was studded with flashing diamonds. She was seated in an armchair by the fire, and Alexander was standing before her. They were laughing about something, but broke off as Elizabeth came in.

Alexander came to greet her, smiling into her eyes as he raised her hand to his lips. 'I trust you are refreshed and in good appetite?'

'I believe I am,' she replied, returning the smile.

Isobel looked away into the fire, struggling to conceal her resentment that Elizabeth had joined them. Her feelings toward Alexander had not wavered at all, indeed if anything they had increased. She was no longer foolish enough to believe him to be a Childe Harold, but this realization had not made any difference. She knew now that she loved him for his own sake, and this hardened her determination more than ever. She still intended to do all she could to take him from her cousin, whose conduct during today's journey could scarcely have been more uninterested. Elizabeth didn't deserve to keep him, she didn't deserve to at all . . . Isobel drew a long breath. She must tread very carefully and very cleverly, and she must always bear in mind Aunt Avery's sage advice that the key to a gentleman's heart was to always make him feel good in one's company. Let Elizabeth's attitude speak for itself, while she, Isobel, was subtly captivating and flattering to be with.

The roast pork dinner proved to be everything the boastful landlord had said it would be, and he had even managed to find a bottle of very good French wine to accompany it. Isobel continued to be charming company, and once again Elizabeth found her thoughts wandering, with the result that she hardly entered into the conversation. She did not notice Alexander's glances beginning to become a little irritated, nor did she observe Isobel's barely concealed delight with the way things were going. It wasn't until almost the end of the meal that Alexander suddenly said something that brought her back sharply to the present, and her own shortcomings.

'Would you prefer to retire now, Elizabeth?'

Elizabeth looked at him in astonishment. 'I . . . I beg your pardon?'

'I asked you if you would rather retire now.' His tone was clipped.

'Why are you being so—?'

'Because I have just addressed you three times to no avail.'

Her lips parted, and she glanced away for a moment before putting her napkin on the table and getting up. 'You are right to chastise me. I fear I am not myself tonight, so perhaps it would be best if I did retire.' She inclined her head, and left the room.

Alexander quickly followed, and caught her arm in the passage outside. 'Elizabeth, forgive me, I beg of you.'

'What is there to forgive, sir? I have been behaving abominably, and you have pointed out the fact in no uncertain terms. I will now do as you suggest, and take myself off to my room.'

'Please forgive me, for I know I should not have spoken as I did.' He took both her arms, and looked anxiously into her eyes. 'Come back inside, and let us forget that I sinned.'

'I don't think that that would be a good idea now, Alexander. I will retire now, and leave you and Isobel to finish dinner.'

'Am I forgiven?'

She managed a smile. 'There is not a great deal to forgive, Alexander, for I know that I haven't been very forthcoming of late. It will pass, I promise.'

He pulled her a little closer. 'I love you very much,' he said softly, bending his head to kiss her on the lips.

She closed her eyes, wanting to feel so much, but even now there was nothing. Tears stung her eyes suddenly, and she pulled back. 'I . . . I will go now. Good night.'

'Good night.' He watched her as she hurried away along the passage, and then he lowered his glance sadly for a moment before returning to the private room, where Isobel was waiting with secret glee, for things could not have gone better for her had she engineered it.

He resumed his seat, giving her a rueful and contrite smile. 'I must now ask you to forgive me as well, Lady Isobel.'

'Oh, please let us stop being so formal, after all we are

almost family, are we not?' She returned the smile. 'Please call me Isobel, and I will call you Alexander.'

'I do not deserve your kindness, Isobel.'

'If I am perfectly honest with you, Alexander, it is Elizabeth who does not deserve any kindness. You were correct to speak sternly to her, for she has hardly said a word all day, and tonight she has been positively sullen.'

'Oh, not sullen, surely?'

'I know it isn't my place to say anything . . .'

'Yes?'

'I think Elizabeth has been thinking a great deal about James.'

'Oh?' He picked up his glass of wine, swirling the liquid thoughtfully.

'I know that when they first married they were very much in love, and perhaps now, with the betrothal and wedding arrangements approaching, she just cannot help recalling other times.'

'With the result that she will also have to concede that I am not at all like James French, either when he was a saint or a sinner.'

Isobel lowered her lovely eyes eloquently.

Alexander drained his glass, and then sat back with a heavy sigh.

She looked quickly at him again, much affected by the shadow in his eyes, and it was all she could do not to reach out to him there and then. But the time was not yet right. The seed of doubt over Elizabeth had begun to take root, but it still had to flourish properly. . . . She smiled at him. 'Perhaps we should retire now, Alexander, for it has been a long day, and we have another such day ahead of us tomorrow.'

He returned the smile. 'Whatever you wish, Isobel,' he murmured, getting up once more and coming around the table to draw out her chair for her.

As she stood, she paused prettily, before stretching up to kiss him briefly on the cheek. 'Thank you for being so very kind to me, Alexander. I know that my presence is probably making things awkward for you and Elizabeth, given that all is not entirely well between you, but I want you to know that I believe you are entirely the injured party. I am very sorry indeed to see you brought so low, especially when your thoughtfulness has helped me to cope with my anxiety over my father's illness.'

'Your presence hasn't made anything awkward, Isobel, indeed it has probably been beneficial.'

'It has?'

'Yes.'

Her green eyes were lustrous and wide. 'If you were mine, Alexander, I would see to it that I never caused you a moment's doubt or unhappiness.'

He met her gaze for a long moment, and then cleared his throat slightly, going to the door to open it for her.

The faintest of satisfied smiles played upon her lips as she went out past him.

Elizabeth dreamed that night. She was in Madras again, lying naked on her muslin-hung bed waiting for James to come to her. Scented candles lit the room, and exotic blooms nodded against the velvety night sky beyond the windows. She was happy, for James had not yet deceived or hurt her, but was still the loving husband who had won her heart so completely.

The night breeze wafted softly through the silent house, and she heard a light step. She turned her head toward the veranda, and he was there, his hair the brightest of gold in the glow from a lantern. He wore a long silk robe that was tied loosely at the waist, and he smiled as he came toward her. The robe slid softly to the floor, and she gazed at his body, so lean, bronzed, and beautiful, but as she reached up to him, his face changed, and it was no longer James French who came to her, but instead was the stranger who had so recently and enigmatically entered her life.

His skin was warm and firm, and his lips teased and aroused as he kissed her. He drew her body against his, holding her so close that she could feel his heart beating. Wild emotions flared into life, and the blood coursed richly through her veins as she responded eagerly to his touch. She was carried away by desire, as if her flesh was melting into his, and the consummation of passion was all that mattered. She clung to him, loving him with a ferocity that threatened to overcome her. She wanted to cry out his name, but she did not know what name to say. Her lips moved, confusion washed frustratingly over her, and she awoke with a gasp, staring up at the canopy overhead.

A single candle had been left burning on the mantelpiece, and its gentle light moved over the room, keeping the darkest shadows away. The dream was still all around her, and her heart was pounding so much that she could not count its beats. She felt as if her lover had only just left. Her lover. It had not been James with whom she had shared her passionate fantasy, it had been a man she hardly knew, but who had tormented her thoughts from the moment she had first seen him.

Hot color flooded into her cheeks, and she turned to bury her face in the pillows. Feelings she had failed to recognize when awake had become only too recognizable in her dreams. Her heart was betraying her, and it was betraying Alexander as well. She was foolishly close to falling in love with a man with whom she was barely acquainted, and who she would probably never see again.

CHAPTER 8

SHE HAD RECOVERED a little by the time she rose from her bed the following morning. The dream remained uncomfortably real, and she had had to face a disturbing fact about her innermost feelings, but outwardly she appeared herself again.

The intense cold had not relented overnight, and now the sun and blue skies had been replaced by a freezing fog that obscured low yellow-gray clouds. Although it hardly seemed possible, the temperature dropped still more, and by dawn a layer of ice had formed on the inside of the inn windows. The fog trapped the air, so that the smoke of Huntingdon's many chimneys did not escape and could be inhaled with every breath. In the yard the lamps of the stagecoaches were muted by the vapor, and were soon lost as the vehicles drove out into the almost deserted street.

Passengers arriving at the inn complained miserably about the rigors of traveling in such weather, and those who were about to depart did so with great trepidation, especially those unfortunate enough to have only secured outside places.

There wasn't a guest in the dining room who did not eat a large breakfast. New arrivals were made ravenous by the cold, and those soon to set off were determined not to suffer through lack of proper sustenance. No one opted for the customary cold breakfast dishes – ham, boiled beef, or pigeon pie – but there was a great demand for eggs, bacon, beef-steaks, kidneys, hot toast, and muffins, to say nothing of coffee, tea, and various more alcoholic beverages. A constant stream of waiters carried fully laden trays from the kitchens, and then spirited away the dirty crockery afterward. At the sound of the ticket-office bell in the yard, reluctant passengers left the warmth of the inn and prepared to endure their journeys as best they could.

As a nearby church clock struck nine, the two traveling carriages set off once more, driving slowly north through the fog toward Alconbury Hill, and a steady climb up out of the fenlands. A wonderful view was usually visible from the top, but although the ascent took them out of the fog, a thick blanket of white obscured everything below.

They passed through the village of Stilton, famous for its cheeses, and at midday they crossed the River Nene at Wansford, and took refreshment at the Haycock Inn. The fog had lifted a little by now, and it was possible to make fair progress, but it seemed unlikely that they would reach Grantham before nightfall, and instead would have to travel at least an hour in the dark.

For Elizabeth the day was an ordeal; with so much on her mind she found it difficult to be as light-hearted and talkative as Alexander wished. She was in no mood to act as frivolous and carefree as Isobel, and now that she had been forced to face her secret emotions, she found it even more difficult to be warm and affectionate toward Alexander. She was in a quandary, unable to understand the unreasonable emotions that had been aroused within her, and she strove with all her might not only to quell them, but to banish them altogether. It was absolute madness to be drawn so strongly to a man she did not ever expect to meet again, and if she gave in to a fancy that could only be passing, she would then be forfeiting a chance of happiness with Alexander. Before she had commenced all this foolishness, they had been happy and content together. The blame lay with her, and so it was up to her to put it all right again. She would shut out all thoughts of James, and she would certainly endeavor to extinguish her misguided attraction toward a man whose name she did not even know.

Struggling with all these secret problems, she inevitably fell back into a reserve that to Alexander seemed exactly the same as the one of the day before, and of other recent days as well. His glance grew darker as the day went on, and he turned more and more of his attention toward Isobel, who was as captivating and fascinating as she could manage.

It was while they were taking a light meal at the Haycock Inn that Elizabeth realized she had once again been guilty of withdrawing from conversation. Remembering Alexander's justifiable reaction of the evening before, she knew she owed him an apology. As they were leaving the warmth of the inn to return to the waiting carriages, she touched his arm a little hesitantly.

'Alexander? May I have a word with you, please?'

He paused, and Isobel reluctantly walked on toward the carriages. She would much have preferred to linger and hear what was said, but could hardly do so without appearing obvious.

He turned to face Elizabeth. 'A word with me? That will

indeed be a novelty.'

She lowered her eyes. 'I know that I've been too quiet again, but I don't mean to—'

'Then what exactly do you mean, Elizabeth?' he interrupted quietly. 'It's James, isn't it?' he asked then, searching her face.

Guilty color reddened her cheeks. 'No,' she whispered.

'Don't lie to me, Elizabeth, for it's written too large. I know that you were once very happy with him, and that what we have now is not the same, but I cannot compete with a ghost. If you wish to withdraw from the match—'

'No! No, of course I don't.'

'Nor do I, but then neither do I wish to continue when you appear so halfhearted about it. I don't understand you anymore, Elizabeth, and I certainly feel shut out.'

Her eyes stung with tears. 'I'm sorry, Alexander, for the last thing I would ever wish would be to hurt you in any way. Please let us start again, and I promise to behave as I should from now on.'

He nodded slightly. 'Very well.'

She smiled and reached up to kiss him on the cheek, but even as she did so she knew the damage had not been fully repaired. He now doubted her commitment, and she had given a promise that she was no longer certain she could honor.

Isobel had watched carefully from her seat in the carriage; her heart had tightened with alarm when she saw Elizabeth kiss him, but as they approached her she saw that all was still not entirely well. There was a troubled look in his eyes, and Elizabeth seemed, well, almost guilty.

They drove on through the afternoon and, as expected,

they still had some way to go when darkness fell. With it came the fog, obscuring the road ahead, and forcing the coachmen to drive at little more than a walk. They passed through Colsterworth, where the road to Lincoln diverged, and where, if it had not been for Isobel, they would have left the main highway to strike out for Norrington Court.

The carriage lamps barely pierced the gloom, and it was so cold that they felt the chill right through to their bones. The comfort of the Grantham inn seemed very far away indeed as they huddled in their seats. Isobel by now was forced to concede that in her efforts to look elegant and *à la mode*, she had sadly neglected comfort and common sense. Alexander insisted that she put his greatcoat around her shoulders, and Elizabeth informed her that the following day she was to be much more sensible. Too cold to argue, Isobel had meekly promised to obey.

It was not long after that, when they were still several miles short of Grantham, that Elizabeth heard hooves approaching swiftly from behind. At first she thought it was just the second carriage endeavoring to keep them in sight, but then she realized that the sound was of a much lighter vehicle, a phaeton or a gig perhaps. She turned to breathe on the window glass, which was now quite frosted over with the cold and, as she wiped a small area to look out, she saw two new carriage lamps quickly approaching them.

The drum of hooves grew steadily louder as the third vehicle drove smartly past. It was a bright-red curricle with a raised black leather hood, and it was drawn by two high-stepping dapple grays. A gentleman was driving, tooling the team along with consummate ease. She couldn't see his face, and could only make out that he was about Alexander's age, and

99

dressed very well. He didn't glance toward either carriage as he passed, and soon he vanished in the fog ahead of them, the sound of his vehicle dwindling away into the gloom and darkness.

He had long gone when the carriages at last drove into Grantham, making their way down the High Street to their inn, also called the George. As they halted in the yard, they were one-hundred-and-ten miles from London, and still had fifty miles to travel before they reached Southwell Park at the end of the next day. There was such a crush of vehicles seeking refuge from the cold night that their arrival went unnoticed by the landlord, who, like his counterpart in Huntingdon, would have personally welcomed anyone traveling in such fine carriages.

Alexander alighted quickly and assisted Elizabeth down first. She paused to raise the veil on her hat, but he chided her quickly. 'Go straight inside, for it's far too cold to linger out here.'

She did as she was bade, and did not glance around the yard before entering the welcome warmth of the inn. She didn't see the bright-red curricle that had passed them on the road shortly before. It was drawn up at the other side of the yard, and was about to depart with a fresh team between the shafts. The gentleman driving it lowered the reins as he saw her, and then his gaze went swiftly toward Alexander, who was now assisting Isobel out of the carriage.

Isobel seized the opportunity that suddenly presented itself, and pretending to stumble a little she reached out to link her arms quickly around Alexander's neck. With a little cry, she clung to him for a moment, savoring the more than agreeable sensation of being so close to him. His arms went immediately to steady her, and then she looked up ruefully into his eyes.

'How clumsy I am,' she murmured.

'I have you safe now,' he replied, releasing her only very slowly.

A warm flush passed over her, and with his great-coat still around her shoulders she followed Elizabeth into the inn.

The gentleman in the curricle alighted, turning to give the reins to a groom before walking across the yard toward Alexander. 'Sir Alexander Norrington, I believe?' he said, his voice very clear in a lull in the general noise of the yard.

Alexander whirled about, staring at him in surprise. His jaw dropped. 'Marcus? Marcus Sheridan?'

'The very same.' Marcus sketched a bow.

'Good God above, so you *are* back in England!' cried Alexander, seizing his hand and pumping it gladly. 'You've hardly changed at all!'

'On the contrary, I've changed a great deal. To begin with I'm older and a damn sight wiser,' replied the other a little dryly.

'Tom Crichton said he'd seen you, but although we made every inquiry we could we found no trace. How long have you been back?'

'Long enough.'

'You're on your way to Rainworth?'

'Yes. They've been anticipating my return for two months now, so the fires will be lit and the larder well stocked.'

'Will you be there long?'

Marcus looked away. 'I intend to make my stay as brief as possible.'

Alexander was curious, but refrained from pursuing the

matter too closely. 'At least assure me that you will be in London for a while, for it would please me greatly if you could attend my betrothal ball.'

'Ah, yes, you and the delightful Mrs French.'

'So you've heard, have you?'

'A whisper or two.'

Alexander was perplexed. 'Dammit, why haven't you contacted any of us? I would have thought that at least Tom and I merited—'

'I'm rectifying the fault now. Where are you going?'

'Going? Oh, Elizabeth and I are chaperoning her cousin, Lady Isobel Crawford, to Southwell Park. The earl is far from well.' Alexander knew he did not have to identify Isobel's family any further, for Southwell Park and Rainworth Priory were not far from each other, and even after ten years Marcus was certain to know of whom he spoke.

'Lady Isobel Crawford?' asked Marcus with quick interest.

'Yes.'

'Well, I'll be damned . . .'

'Why do you say that?'

'Eh? Oh, nothing.' Marcus shifted his position slightly, shivering a little in the cold. 'If the lady requires a chaperone, and if her name is still Crawford, I take it she is unattached?'

Alexander hesitated. 'Er – yes, she is. Why? Are you seeking a wife?'

Marcus gave a wry smile. 'That, my dear fellow, is very much in the lap of the gods. Alexander, I have a suggestion to make. Southwell Park is near Rainworth, and you will have to pass close by, so why do you not all three stay with me on the way? I take it you mean to continue your journey tomorrow?'

'Yes, but—'

'Stay with me,' Marcus pressed. 'It will not mean much of a delay, and Lady Isobel will be able to see her father the day after if she so desires.'

'Marcus, nothing would please me more, but I think I should consult Elizabeth and Isobel first. Come inside and meet them now.'

'I cannot socialize at the moment, I have a fresh team in harness and must be on my way without delay. I mean to reach Rainworth tonight.'

Alexander's eyes widened with disbelief. 'Tonight? You intend to travel all that way in weather like this? And after dark to boot?'

'That is the general idea,' Marcus confiimed quietly.

'It's madness.'

Marcus smiled. 'Then consider me mad. Well? Is it agreed? Will you and the ladies be my guests tomorrow night?'

Alexander was forced to laugh. 'Oh, very well, it's agreed.'

'Excellent. I will expect you then.' Turning, Marcus strode away again, getting quickly into the curricle and then accepting the reins from the groom before tossing him a coin.

Still a little bemused, Alexander stood watching as the small vehicle drove swiftly out of the busy yard and vanished into the swirling mist of the High Street. There was so much noise all around that he did not hear anything of its departure. He stared after it, almost wondering if he had imagined the encounter, but then he saw the groom walking away, flicking the coin high into the air and then deftly catching it again. The meeting with Marcus hadn't been imagined, it had really happened, and he, Alexander Norrington, had just accepted an invitation that might not meet with the ladies' approval. Isobel wished to see her father without delay, and Elizabeth . . . Well, who knew what Elizabeth would feel.

Alexander sighed, and then turned on his heel to go into the lamplit inn.

Almost immediately he saw Isobel coming down the staircase toward him carrying a lighted candlestick, since it was dark on the floor above. It was by design and not accident that she was there, for when she and Elizabeth had been conducted to their rooms, she had waited until she heard Elizabeth's door close, and had then hastened back to wait at the top of the staircase, intent upon stealing a moment or so alone with him. She hurried toward him in a rustle of emerald-green silk.

'Wherever have you been, Alexander?' she asked, linking her arm with his as if it were the most natural thing in the world.

His hand rested briefly over hers on his sleeve. 'The strangest thing has just happened, Isobel. I've just been speaking to Marcus Sheridan.'

'Sheridan? The only Sheridans I know of are the playwright Member of Parliament, and the Dukes of Arlingham, and the latter are extinct.' She smiled at him.

'Not extinct at all.' He briefly explained about Marcus.

'And chance brought you together here in Grantham? How very odd.'

'Isobel, he has invited us all to stay with him at Rainworth tomorrow night, and he was so insistent that I'm afraid I accepted. I do hope you are not angry with me.'

'Angry with you? Why would I be angry?' Nothing could please her more than the prospect of another night during which to further her plans.

'I was thinking of your wish to see your father as quickly as possible.'

'Oh.' She lowered her eyes quickly, but then smiled at him again. 'It will only be for a short while, and I would not dream of spoiling your opportunity to see your friend after all this time. Please do not think I'm offended in any way.'

He looked warmly into her face. 'You are quite wonderful, Isobel, and the man who snaps you up will be a very fortunate fellow indeed.'

'I am flattered you should think so, Alexander,' she breathed, trying to make her eyes as wide and lustrous as possible.

'Perhaps Marcus will be the lucky man.'

'Marcus?' She drew back, her smile a little fixed.

'I have reason to believe he is looking for a bride, and he was certainly very interested in you.'

'Indeed.' The word was not uttered inquiringly, but in a flat tone that discouraged any further comment on the subject of Marcus Sheridan's marital intentions.

Alexander knew that this time he had definitely offended her. 'Forgive me, for I spoke out of turn.'

'Yes, you did.' She looked crossly away.

'I was paying you a compliment, for I cannot imagine that any man would be indifferent to you.'

She raised her eyes slowly to his face again. 'Do you mean that, Alexander?'

'Of course I do.'

She held his gaze. 'Would you pay court to me if you were free?'

For a long moment he did not reply, but then he nodded. 'Yes, I would.'

Her heart almost missed a beat, and her fingers tightened a little on his sleeve. 'Then I shall have to hope that Elizabeth casts you off, shall I not?' she murmured lightly, smiling as if she jested.

He returned the smile a little uncertainly. 'There may be more truth in that than you think,' he replied.

'What do you mean?' she asked quickly, her heart not simply seeming to skip a beat, but to stop beating altogether.

'I mean that I am no longer sure if she loves me.'

It was difficult not to show exultation at such a revelation, but somehow Isobel contrived to look concerned and sympathetic. 'I am sure you must be wrong, for no sensible woman would ever stop loving you, Alexander. *I* would certainly never stop.'

'You are very good for my morale and vanity, Isobel,' he replied, hesitating and then putting his hand to her cheek.

She gazed breathlessly up at him, a confession of love trembling on her lips. Was now the moment? Should she show herself in her true colors?

Alexander's hand fell away, and he glanced toward the staircase. 'Is she in her room now?'

Disappointment sliced through Isobel. She had missed an opportunity, and now it was too late. 'Er – yes. We have been given rooms on the same floor. Come on, I'll show you the way.' Taking his hand, and holding the candlestick to light the way, she led him up the staircase. Still holding his hand, she drew him along the dark passageway at the top. The candle flames flared and smoked, their dancing light shining in her eyes as she halted at Elizabeth's door.

'This is her room, mine is that one over there, and I believe that yours is the last one on the left at the end of the passage.' She smiled. 'I am sure that Elizabeth will not mind about tomorrow night, and I am also sure that you must be wrong about her affections.'

'I would be a happy man if I could be as sure about anything where she is concerned of late. I do not know where I am with her.' He glanced toward the door.

'I will leave you,' she said quickly. 'The same dinner arrangements have been made as were made at Huntingdon last night, except that this time I believe we are to be served roast beef.' With another smile she turned and walked away toward her own room. He could not see, but she had her fingers secretly crossed, hoping with all her heart that Elizabeth was difficult about the visit to Rainworth Priory, and that he was correct to fear a withdrawal of love. Oh, *please* let both be so, and let Elizabeth herself break things off!

Alexander knocked at the door. 'Elizabeth? It's me.'

'Oh, please come in, Alexander,' she called from inside.

The room was very much like the one in Huntingdon, except that it overlooked the busy yard and the bed was draped with faded crimson velvet. Elizabeth was seated at the dressing table in the sky-blue marguerite gown, and Violet was just putting the finishing touches to her coiffure.

Her smile faded a little as she saw the uncomfortable look on his face. 'Is something wrong?' she asked quickly, waving Violet away.

'I have a confession to make,' he said as the door closed behind the maid.

Elizabeth rose to her feet. 'A confession? What about?'

He explained what had happened. 'I know I should not have accepted like that, but I did, and now Marcus expects us tomorrow evening,' he finished.

'It is done, and that is the end of it,' she said, carefully keeping the dismay from her voice. She did not want another

107

delay, she wanted everything to be accomplished so that they could reach the haven of Norrington Court and she could begin to repair the damage that had been done to their relationship. The longer things went on as they were, the worse it would become.

He smiled with relief. 'Then you do not mind?'

'No, of course not.'

He pulled her into his arms, but as he kissed her it was another of whom she thought, another for whose lips she yearned.

CHAPTER 9

ELIZABETH ROSE AT half-past seven the following morning, before it was really light and, as she looked out of her window at the busy yard, she saw immediately that the fog had lifted. Glancing up at the sky, she noted how gray and lowering it seemed to be. Such clouds could only herald the long-antici-pated snow.

She gazed at the sky in dismay. If it snowed a great deal they might find themselves stranded at Rainworth. Oh, plague take Marcus Sheridan for inviting them there, for she had no desire at all to enjoy his hospitality. She drew a long breath then. What was done was done, and if she wished to put matters right with Alexander, then she must make the best of it. She was ashamed of her recent conduct, and felt almost as if she really had deceived him. But she had not, and she would not, because she loved him very much, and today she would be everything she should be to him. By the time they reached Rainworth he would no longer have any reason to be displeased or disappointed with her behavior.

The resolve was still as strong when Violet came to assist her to dress, and had not wavered at all by the time she went down to join the others in the crowded dining room. She greeted Alexander warmly, and her breakfast conversation could not have been faulted. She was lighthearted, amusing, witty, and attentive, but in truth it was an acting tour de force, for deep inside she remained as unsure and unhappy as she had been before. It was one thing to tell herself how she should feel and behave, quite another to be those things.

Their breakfast was as substantial as had been the one taken in Huntingdon, for they still had to be mindful of the cold and of the hours that would pass before they stopped for luncheon. Now they also had to take account of the possibility of snow, for everyone in the dining room felt that it would not be long in coming. At just after nine, with everyone dressed in their warmest clothes – even Isobel – they set off toward Rainworth.

This time the two carriages did not continue north as before, but headed west, following the Nottingham road as it led through the beautiful Vale of Belvoir, where Belvoir Castle presided over the countryside from its rocky crag to the south of the road. The ancestral home of the Dukes of Rutland was well named, as indeed was the whole area, for the view in all directions was beautiful indeed, even in the depths of such a winter.

To Isobel's impotent fury, Elizabeth maintained her new leaf, not allowing her attention to wander for even a short while. Isobel could only seethe in silence as she saw how Alexander responded to his future wife. Oh, this was too bad! And just when it had seemed that things were going all her, Isobel's, way. Isobel glowered up at Belvoir Castle, her mind racing as she wondered how to deal with this irritatingly recovered Elizabeth. She would have to think of something, for she only had today and tonight left before they reached Southwell Park. Perhaps drastic action would be required.

It began to snow just as the little Nottinghamshire market town of Bingham came into view ahead. Large crisp flakes fell swiftly from the skies, and soon began to form a thin carpet of white on the ground. At Bingham they left the Nottingham road, striking northwest toward the rolling vista of Sherwood Forest, which was just visible on the far horizon when they stopped for luncheon at an inn on the bank of the deep, swift-flowing River Trent.

Isobel had little appetite for the inn's succulent beefsteak pie, and only picked at it as she gazed out at the snow, which still fell heavily over the entire countryside. Let it fall and fall, let it block all the roads overnight and force them to stay on at Rainworth. Yes, that was what she prayed now, so that she would have more opportunity to further her designs upon Alexander.

She had had hardly any chance to claim his attention so far today, for Elizabeth had been in sparkling form, giving her secret rival no opening at all in which to try to reassert herself. An opening did appear, however, leaving Isobel alone with Alexander for a minute or so before they returned to the carriages for the last part of the journey to Rainworth. Isobel was not slow to act.

She looked a little reproachfully at him. 'Have I said something wrong?' she asked in a small voice.

His lips parted in surprise. 'Wrong? Why, no, of course not. Why ever do you ask such a thing?'

'Because you've barely spoken to me today.'

He stared at her. 'Oh, Isobel, if I have neglected you then I am deeply sorry.' He instinctively took her hand, raising it to his lips.

Her green eyes were still large and reproachful. 'I have been feeling quite wretched, for I was sure I must have done something to offend you.'

'Never think that,' he said softly, still holding her hand by cupping it in both of his.

'What am I supposed to think when you devote your complete attention to Elizabeth, and leave me all on my own?'

'I promise not to be negligent again. Please forgive me.'

Her lips trembled a little, and unshed tears shimmered in her eyes. 'Of course I forgive you,' she whispered.

He was about to say something more when Elizabeth returned to join them, and he swiftly released Isobel's hand. They went out into the snow to climb back into the waiting carriages, and a moment later were on their way once more.

The snow did not relent, but continued to fall heavily. The team's hooves now made little sound, and there were fewer and fewer travelers on the road as most wisely took shelter rather than risk becoming snowbound on the highway. Rainworth was only about two hours ahead now, a long way in such conditions, but they were confident that they would reach their destination before the roads became too bad and daylight faded.

Sherwood Forest seemed to fold silently over them, its bare-branched oak trees interspersed here and there with dark green pines and other evergreens. The snow lay deep and white, and fell with an endless monotony that foretold of inevitably blocked roads. Isobel looked out with hidden delight, unable to help stealing a surreptitious glance at Alexander as he sat opposite her. His gaze was already upon her, and he smiled. She smiled back.

Elizabeth was looking out at the snow as well, but with increasing dismay. The prospect of being snow-bound at Rainworth loomed ever nearer.

The carriages pressed farther and farther into Robin Hood's forest, and as the afternoon began to draw in there was still no sign of an end to the snow. Progress became steadily more slow, and the only consolation was that the immense carpet of white staved off the darkness for a little longer than would otherwise have been the case. The horses made no sound except for their snorting breaths and the jingle of their harness as they made what speed they could along the now deserted road. As daylight at last began to fade, they paused for the carriage lamps to be lit before driving on again. Rainworth could not be far ahead now.

They passed the entrance of Lord Byron's country seat, Newstead Abbey, but Isobel did not even glance at it. Neither the poet nor his works were of any interest to her now, for she was too rapt in her feelings for Alexander as he really was, not as she had imagined him to be. She no longer gave a fig for Childe Harold, and the once treasured volume of the *Pilgrimage* had not even been taken out of the overnight valise since leaving London.

At long last the stone gateposts of Rainworth appeared in the arc of pale light from the carriage lamps. The handsome wrought-iron gates stood open, and the drive beyond plunged down into a long valley where snow-laden rhododendrons marked the way. The relieved coachmen negotiated the turn and set the weary horses down the drive, which curved away into the darkness ahead, passing through a gracious park that had been stolen from the surrounding forest.

There were no lights ahead to show that they were close to the house, and it seemed almost as if the drive had no end, when suddenly it curved away to the left again, and the house swung into view. It was too dark to see the outline of the walls and roof, but the lighted windows showed it to indeed be partly a medieval priory, for they were made of stained glass and were gracefully arched and traceried.

As the teams were finally halted next to a wide flight of stone steps that led up to the main entrance, the door of the house was flung open and some footmen carrying lighted flambeaux hastened out to attend to their master's guests. Elizabeth felt the icy touch of snowflakes upon her face as she accepted Alexander's hand to alight, and the moment Isobel had stepped down from the carriage as well, they were conducted up the steps into the house. Their servants followed, again carrying the overnight valises.

Rainworth had ceased to be a priory in the sixteenth century, having fallen victim to the harsh attentions of King Henry VIII, and on its dissolution it had been purchased by the Sheridan family, who had turned it into a magnificent Tudor mansion, with a vast baronial hall as the main entrance. It possessed a lofty hammer beam ceiling and the walls were paneled with ancient Sherwood oak. There was a raised dais to one side, with a minstrels' gallery above it, and directly opposite the doors there rose a grand staircase with carved lion newel posts.

On the walls were tapestries depicting scenes from the legend of Robin Hood, and there was also an extensive display of weaponry, from medieval battleaxes and pikes, to dueling pistols and sporting guns from a more recent age. A number of suits of armor stood against the walls, several of them highly decorative and obviously made of silver, and there was a full-size figure of a knight mounted on a courser, the horse richly caparisoned in crimson-and-gold, the knight himself splendid in tournament armor with white plumes springing from the lion crest on his helmet. The lion emblem appeared everywhere, on the oak paneling and the staircase, around the immense stone fireplace, and in the stained glass of the line of windows high on the wall above the main entrance, for it had always been the heraldic badge of the Dukes of Arlingham.

In daytime the windows provided ample light, but now that it was dark outside the mansion was lit by a line of six wheel-rimmed chandeliers suspended from the hammer beams. Each chandelier possessed a score of candles, which cast a rich glow over the hall, their flames reflected in the long polished oak table ranging down the center of the stone floor. Twenty Tudor chairs were in place around the table and there were more such chairs on either side of the fireplace, where tall flames flickered brightly around fresh logs. It seemed that whenever balls or other musical entertainments were held, the orchestra did not play from the minstrels' gallery, but rather from the dais below it, where there stood a graceful gilded harp and a grand piano inlaid with ebony and mother-of-pearl. Isobel was delighted to see the piano, for she was a very accomplished player, and it seemed a very fine instrument indeed. She resolved to play it before their stay was over.

A splendidly attired butler was waiting to greet them. He wore a brown velvet coat with gold embroidery on the collar and cuffs, beige silk breeches and stockings, and black shoes with golden buckles. Wisps of sandy hair peeped from beneath his bag-wig. He was about forty-five years old, with a pale freckled face and light-blue eyes. When he spoke it was with a Scottish accent that again brought James to Elizabeth's mind.

'Welcome to Rainworth,' he said. 'His Grace extends his sincere regrets, but he has been called out very urgently to a barn fire at the Home Farm. He left instructions that the house was to be placed entirely at your disposal, and wishes to assure you that he will return in time to dine at eight.'

Alexander nodded at him. 'It cannot be helped, er—' He waited for the butler to give his name.

'McPherson, sir.'

'McPherson. Well, if we could be conducted to our rooms, and perhaps be served some light refreshment, we will gladly await the duke's return.'

'Very well, Sir Alexander. Your rooms are ready and waiting, and I will see that tea is served without delay.'

The butler turned, beckoning to three maids who had been waiting in the shadows by the staircase. They picked up some lighted candles from a small table concealed in an alcove, and then stepped forward to conduct the guests to their accommodation.

As Elizabeth, Isobel, and their own maids, followed two of them up the staircase, McPherson delayed Alexander for a moment.

'Begging your pardon, Sir Alexander, but may I suggest that it might be wise to unload all your luggage from the carriages? With the snow falling as heavily as it is, I do not believe you will be able to leave in the morning, and possibly not for days yet. You and the ladies might be glad of the use of all your clothing and so on. . . ?'

'I think you may be right, McPherson. Very well, please see that everything is brought in.'

'Sir.'

Alexander then followed the third maid, and as he did so the butler instructed footmen to attend to the carriages.

From the top of the staircase, Elizabeth and Isobel had entered a long gallery lined on one side with tall windows overlooking the original cloisters. The other wall, which was paneled like the hall, bore a collection of portraits, mostly of former members of the Sheridan family, but with a sprinkling of royalty here and there, notably Charles I and Queen Henrietta-Maria. Evidently the Dukes of Arlingham had remained staunchly royalist throughout the civil war.

A number of doors opened off the gallery, each one draped on either side with heavy dark-green velvet curtains, and at the far end there were two passages, one leading to the right and back into the Tudor portion of the house, the other to the left, into the heart of the old priory. Isobel and her maid were conducted along the former, Elizabeth and Violet along the latter.

The maid protected the candle flame with her hand as she led Elizabeth along a stone way. There was no oak paneling now, just bare stone, and the doors that opened off on either side were iron-studded and set in arches.

After entering a farther passage, the maid paused. 'Please take care here, Lady Isobel, for there are some very steep steps.'

'I will take care, but I have to point out that I am not Lady Isobel,' replied Elizabeth.

The maid stared at her, her glance flickering briefly to the dark-blond curls that were visible around her forehead. 'Not

Lady Isobel?' she repeated.

'No. I am Mrs French.'

'Oh, but I thought . . .' The maid fell silent. Elizabeth was curious. 'Does my identity make any difference?' she inquired.

'Er – no, of course not, madam. I have made a mistake, that's all.' Turning, the maid went carefully down the steps, her candle flaring and smoking for a moment in an unseen draft before she remembered to protect the flame with her hand again.

They followed the passage around what appeared to be the foot of a tower, and then passed a door at the top of three well-worn stone steps. The room beyond was in the tower. The passage continued a short way and ended with another iron-studded door set in an archway.

The maid paused at the steps of the tower door and pointed toward the other door at the end. 'That leads outside, madam. There is a terrace, and then some steps leading down through the gardens to the lake.'

'There is a lake?'

'Oh, yes, madam. You drove right past it when you arrived, but it's been frozen over for several weeks now, and the ice will be covered with snow, so that you could not possibly have seen it in the dark. Please come this way.' She went up the steps, and opened the door at the top, hurrying swiftly inside to light some candles.

Elizabeth was agreeably surprised by the sumptuous scene that greeted her. The stone walls could have appeared bare and austere, but they flickered with light from the candles and the fire; they were hung with jewel-bright tapestries depicting scenes from romantic legends. On the floor there

118

was a carpet woven with lions and roses, and through an archway there was another small room, evidently a dressing-room, for Elizabeth glimpsed a modern dressing table draped with frilled white muslin.

The bed was a very large and ancient four-poster, with a lavish canopy of gold-fringed plum velvet, and curtains of the same velvet were drawn across the two arched windows. There was a tall carved armchair beside the fire, its design reminiscent of a medieval throne, and in an alcove there was an old cabinet with doors adorned with the Sheridan coat-of-arms.

'Do you require anything, madam?' asked the maid.

'No, that will be all, thank you. Oh, yes, one thing . . .'

'Madam?'

'I gather that dinner will be served at eight, but since I have no idea where the dining-room is. . . ?'

'A footman will come to conduct you to the grand chamber, madam. It is the custom for guests to gather there before proceeding to the prior's parlor, which is the name given to the dining-room.'

Bobbing a curtsy, the maid picked up her candlestick and withdrew from the room.

Elizabeth glanced around again and then slowly took the pins from her hat before removing it from her head and hand-ing it to Violet. Then she went to the nearest of the windows and drew aside the heavy plum velvet curtains. There was a tapestry-upholstered window seat in the embrasure beyond, and an arched window with diamond-shaped panes of glass, which were opaque with a frosting of ice. Kneeling on the seat, she breathed upon the ice, then quickly wiped the pane in order to look out.

Countless snowflakes fluttered silently down through the darkness, illuminated briefly by the candlelight in the room behind her. It seemed the weather was relentlessly determined to keep them here at Rainworth for more than just the one night.

In her room in another part of the house, Isobel was also looking out of the window. She could hear Alexander and his man talking in the next room, for the two chambers had originally been one large one and were now divided only by wooden paneling. A smile played upon her lips as she gazed at the snow. Let them be immured here for days. . . .

CHAPTER 10

THE TIME APPROACHED to go down to the grand chamber before dinner, and Elizabeth's preparations were almost complete as she sat at the dressing table for Violet to carefully tease the final curl into place.

It had proved a welcome and unexpected diversion to be able to choose from all the clothes she had brought from London, and she had decided upon a gown made of lavender Spanish merino. It had a low square neckline, a silver draw-string at the high waist immediately beneath her breasts, and there was silver embroidery on the hem and little puffed sleeves. With it she intended to carry a warm white grenadine shawl with knotted ends that would swing when she moved.

Her hair was dressed up into a tumble of little curls on top of her head and was fixed in place with a tall silver comb. She wore silver-and-amethyst earrings, and a matching necklace, and she was pleased with her reflection in the little looking glass on the dressing table. Dabbing a little lavender water behind her ears, she got up and shook out the skirt of her gown.

'You look lovely, madam,' Violet said admiringly before

beginning to put away the unused pins.

'I hope so,' Elizabeth replied with feeling, for tonight she had to continue making up for her recent failings. 'Do you know if the duke has returned yet?'

'He had not when I came up from the kitchens, madam.'

'I wonder what he's like?' Elizabeth mused, for Marcus Sheridan was still something of a mystery.

'All the maids here think he is the most handsome gentleman in all the world. They're all sighing over him.'

'Indeed?'

Violet nodded. 'The maid who showed us here to this room told me all the gossip below stairs, madam.'

'Gossip? About the duke?'

'Yes, madam. It seems he was heard telling Mr McPherson that he intends to sell Rainworth and then return to America. I believe there is a lady he intends to marry.'

Elizabeth stared at her. 'He actually means to sell Rainworth?'

'That is what they are saying, madam.'

'But it is his heritage, his family have lived here for hundreds of years!'

'Yes, madam.'

Elizabeth did not say anything more, for she could not imagine that anyone would voluntarily sell a house like this, but would only do so if in financial straits.

The footman came to conduct her to the grand chamber, and after pulling her shawl comfortably around her shoulders, she followed him back the way the maid had brought her earlier. The grand chamber opened off the main entrance hall, and so Elizabeth found herself retracing her steps exactly, walking along the gallery above the cloisters, and then emerging at the top of the staircase. She was about to descend behind the footman when she heard someone hailing the house outside, and she stopped instinctively, her hand resting on the topmost lion newel post.

The outer door burst open, and a cloaked gentleman strode in, his spurred top boots leaving snowy prints on the stone floor. His face was hidden by his tall-crowned hat, which was pulled low over his forehead, and he brushed snow from the shoulders as he called impatiently for the butler.

'McPherson? Where are you, dammit? I need someone to attend my horse!'

'I'm here, Your Grace, and someone is already going to see to your horse,' the butler answered, hurrying from somewhere behind the staircase, almost directly below where Elizabeth stood.

She stared down at the cloaked gentleman. So this was Marcus Sheridan, eighth Duke of Arlingham. She waited for him to remove his hat so that she could see his face, but he did not do so immediately.

McPherson assisted him with his cloak first. 'Is all well at the Home Farm now, Your Grace?'

'Yes, it wasn't as great a fire as seemed at first. Are they here yet?'

'Yes, Your Grace, they arrived just after nightfall.'

'And all is well?' Marcus turned for the butler to remove his cloak. Beneath it he wore a very stylish gray-blue riding coat and close-fitting beige breeches. A full neckcloth frothed at his throat, and the frills of his shirt pushed through his partially buttoned rose marcella waistcoat. He was every inch a gentleman of taste and fashion.

At last he removed his hat, and as he did so Elizabeth gave

a sharp intake of breath, drawing swiftly back out of sight at the top of the staircase. Marcus Sheridan, Duke of Arlingham, was none other than her mysterious rescuer, the man she had seen leaving the house in Hanover Square, and the man with whom she had dreamed of making such passionate and abandoned love!

Her pulse quickened with shock, and she felt embarrassed color flooding into her cheeks, for in those few brief moments she felt almost as if he would know what she had dreamed simply by looking into her eyes. She pressed her trembling hands to her face, willing the telltale blush to fade away again. She closed her eyes, struggling to compose herself. Oh, this was the end in foolishness! Her dreams were private, and she had not confided in anyone, so how could he possibly know?

She swallowed, trying to steady the almost panic-stricken emotion that rushed through her, and then she emerged from the shadows to peep down into the hall again.

The footman who had been conducting her to the grand chamber had halted halfway down the staircase, and was looking back at her in puzzlement. He did not know why she had drawn back out of sight, and so he could only wait for her to decide what to do.

She hardly noticed the footman, for her gaze was solely on Marcus as he teased off his gloves and dropped them into his upturned hat. He was speaking to McPherson about the extent of the fire damage at the Home Farm, and as he smiled suddenly she was struck anew by how exceedingly handsome he was.

His golden hair was ruffled and the raw cold outside had brought a healthy glow to his cheeks. The deep blue of his eyes was discernible even from where she stood, and there was something so compelling about him that she could only stare. He reminded her keenly of James, of the first James, the one she had loved so very much, and yet at the same time he was very different. His mannerisms were not the same, for where James had been quick and almost nervous, Marcus Sheridan was confident and self-assured.

Suddenly, almost as if he sensed she was there, he looked directly up at her. Their eyes met. For a long moment he did not move, but then he strode toward the foot of the staircase.

Her senses were in turmoil as she went down to meet him, and she trusted that she appeared to be more calm and composed than she felt. Please do not let her emotion show on her face. . . . Seeing him again so unexpectedly had shaken her so much that she did not know what to say. A subtle and dangerous air of excitement now pervaded her, and memories of her sensuous dream had begun to coil around her again.

As she reached him at the bottom of the staircase, he took her hand, drawing it gently to his lips. Frissons of pleasure shivered secretly over her as she strove to seem collected and at ease. She could smell the winter night on his clothes, and feel it in his touch, but there was nothing cold in his glance or smile as he greeted her.

'We meet again,' he said softly.

'I . . . I don't quite know what to say, for I did not expect to find that *you* are my host.'

'I confess to having been taken equally by surprise when I saw you alight from Alexander's carriage in Grantham, and I am sorry that I did not feel able to speak to you properly then, but I had fresh horses in harness and waiting—'

'There is no need to apologize, Your Grace.'

'But there is, for I realize that I have more or less forced my hospitality upon you.' He smiled a little contritely. 'I am glad that you are here, however, for I now have the opportunity to return your property.'

Her lips parted. 'My earrings? You managed to retrieve them?'

'I relieved certain uncouth gentlemen of their ill-gotten gains, yes, and I will return them to you before you leave.'

She lowered her eyes. 'I am truly sorry that I did not wait in the lane as you requested, but we thought we heard the footpads returning, and I am afraid we took fright.' Oh, how handsome he was, and how much at sixes and sevens she was set by his smile and the softness in his voice.

'Please do not apologize, Lady Isobel, for it is quite under-standable under the circumstances.'

She was startled, for this was the second time since arriving here that she had been taken for her cousin. 'Your Grace, I am not Lady Isobel, I am Elizabeth French.'

He stared at her and then drew perceptibly back, running his fingers through his blond hair. 'Not Lady Isobel?' he repeated.

'No.'

'I appear to have made an error,' he murmured.

'A simple enough error.'

'Or the error of a simpleton,' he said, almost as an aside. 'It's just that when I saw you go into the inn, and then saw how . . .'

'Yes?'

'It – er – doesn't matter, Mrs French, for the fact remains that I have confused you with Lady Isobel.'

His reaction made her curious, for of what consequence was such a mistake? What difference did it make whether she was Isobel or not? The only difference that sprang immediately to mind was that Isobel was unmarried and eligible, but that could hardly be the reason for his response, for belowstairs gossip told of his intention to marry a lady in America. So, why was he so disturbed about having taken her for her cousin? 'Is something wrong, Your Grace? Does it matter that I am not Lady Isobel?'

'Matter? No, of course not,' he replied, giving her a quick smile, but avoiding meeting her eyes for more than the most fleeting of moments.

It was plain to her that it did matter, and equally plain that he did not intend to explain why.

He smiled again, and she could almost feel the change in him, for where he had been open and warm before, he was now reserved and almost cool. 'Please allow the footman to conduct you to the grand chamber, Mrs French, for if Alexander and Lady Isobel are not already there, I am sure they will join you shortly.' Inclining his head, he stepped deliberately aside for her to pass.

A little bewildered, she nodded and then gathered her skirts to step from the staircase and walk toward the footman, who had withdrawn to a discreet distance while she and Marcus talked. The footman bowed to her and then continued to walk across the vast hall toward the far end, where double doors studded with iron were set in a tall stone archway.

She glanced back, and saw that Marcus remained where he was. His gaze was upon her, and he did not look away as she looked back. Then the footman opened the double doors, and she stepped into the brightly lit chamber beyond. The footman closed the doors behind her.

The grand chamber, which had originally been the priory refectory, was magnificently furnished with a suite of seventeenth-century Flemish furniture upholstered with Beauvais tapestry. Dark-green velvet curtains were drawn across the high windows, and the original stone walls had been paneled to match the hall. There were several Boulle cabinets, various tables and chairs, and more highly polished suits of armor, as well as a display of dueling pistols on one wall and a collection of fencing foils on another. Wheel-rimmed chandeliers were suspended from the high-beamed ceiling, and there was an immense stone fireplace where once the monks' meals had been cooked.

Isobel was seated on a chair close to the fire. She wore a yellow-and-white-striped silk gown that looked perfect with her dark chestnut hair, and there was a pale green shawl over her arms, so that once again she looked very light and summery for such a raw and inhospitable January night. She did not observe Elizabeth enter, and was smiling up at something Alexander was saying.

He stood nearby with his back to the fire. His indigo coat was burnished to purple by the flames behind him, and the flickering light caught on the diamond pin in his neckcloth as he turned slightly toward Isobel to say whatever it was that made her smile.

Then Isobel saw Elizabeth approaching, and quickly snapped open her fan. 'Hello again, Elizabeth. How lovely you look. Lavender becomes you very well indeed, does it not, Alexander?'

'Yes, it does,' he replied, coming toward Elizabeth and taking her hand, drawing it palm-uppermost to his lips.

She was still a little distracted after her encounter with Marcus, and it must have shown in her expression, for he looked at her in concern.

'Is something wrong?' he asked quickly, cupping her hand in both his.

'Wrong? No, of course not, it's just that strange coincidences would appear to be the order of the day at the moment.' She explained about Marcus.

Alexander stared at her. 'You mean that Marcus Sheridan is your Sir Galahad?'

'Yes, and he managed to regain my earrings for me. I still cannot really believe it. I was just about to come down the staircase when in walked the very gentleman who had come to my rescue in Kensington! It really is quite remarkable.'

Alexander gave a pleased and slightly disbelieving laugh. 'First of all he spots me in Grantham, and now this. You're right, coincidence does indeed seem to be the order of the day.' Smiling, he conducted her to a chair opposite Isobel, who immediately leaned forward almost conspiratorily.

'What is our host like, Elizabeth? I am most curious to learn about him, for I have been hearing servants' whispers. First of all, is he as devastatingly handsome as I am told?'

'He is,' replied Elizabeth, glancing across at her and wondering again why Marcus had been so concerned to learn of the mistaken identity. 'What gossip have you been hearing?' she inquired.

'Oh, simply that he intends to sell this estate and then return to America to marry.' Isobel's green eyes were wide as they turned toward Alexander. 'So you see, your friend Marcus cannot possibly have designs upon me.'

Elizabeth looked quickly from one to the other. 'Designs

upon you? Why do you say that?'

'Well, when Alexander met the duke in Grantham, it seems inquiries were made concerning my status, and Alexander is convinced that such interest as to whether I was married or not might indicate an intention to pay court to me.'

Alexander colored a little, remembering how offended she had been when he'd mentioned it. 'Well, it seemed like that at the time,' he muttered.

'Unless your friend intends to have two duchesses, then it cannot possibly be so,' replied Isobel.

'He didn't mention anything about a future wife in America. In fact, when I come to think of it, he wasn't very forthcoming about anything and was actually a little secretive. No doubt all will be revealed, for our presence is going to be foisted upon him for several days I fear.'

Isobel nodded, wafting her fan to-and-fro. 'Yes, I fear so too,' she murmured, concealing a satisfied smile. She studied Elizabeth for a moment, wondering why she was so flustered at the discovery of who their host was. She was more than a little ruffled, almost as if she had been caught out in something. But what? If it had not been that Elizabeth had quite definitely not known the identity of her gentleman rescuer, Isobel would have suspected her of a brief dalliance behind Alexander's back. Oh, if only that were so, for it would assist greatly in salving her own conscience, which was becoming a little guilty.

The doors opened again, and McPherson entered with a silver tray upon which stood a crystal decanter and several small glasses. The decanter contained a pale golden liquid, which he poured into the glasses the moment he had placed the tray on a table.

Alexander accepted his glass, and looked curiously at the drink. 'What is it, McPherson?' he asked.

'It is a liqueur that has always been made here at Rainworth, Sir Alexander, and it has always been the tradition to take a glass before dinner.'

Elizabeth sipped her glass. It was sweet and slightly herbal, as if made from the flowers and young oak leaves of Sherwood. She reflected that it was very sad that Marcus should apparently be considering selling an ancestral home that was so full of tradition.

They were still drinking the liqueur when Marcus joined them at last. He was very elegant in black velvet, with a pale blue satin waistcoat and a sapphire pin on the knot of his starched cravat. Lace frills spilled from the front of his shirt and from his cuffs, and he looked quite graceful and distinguished as he executed a stylish bow.

'Please forgive me for not having been here when you arrived, and for being rather late now. I trust that McPherson has been attending to your needs?'

Alexander grinned at him. 'You are forgiven, my friend. Come, allow me to introduce you to Lady Isobel. Mrs French I believe you already know.'

Marcus's blue eyes were turned very briefly toward Elizabeth. 'Yes, we've met,' he murmured.

Isobel extended her hand, smiling up into his eyes. 'I am delighted to make your acquaintance, Your Grace.'

'And I yours, Lady Isobel,' he said, raising her hand to his lips and returning the smile. 'I am already acquainted with your parents, at least I was some years ago, but I do not believe that you and I have ever met.'

'I doubt that we did, sir, for when last you were here I

would have been confined to my school-room.'

'Please do not remind me of how time marches ever onward, Lady Isobel,' he replied, smiling again, then turning to accept a glass of the liqueur from McPherson, who had waited discreetly by the table.

Alexander resumed his place before the hearth. 'I trust that the farm fire was extinguished without too much damage?'

'It was caught in time. There was a danger of losing a barn and all the hay stored there, but we managed to douse the flames before they took too great a hold. The loss of a hay store in weather like this would have been a serious blow.'

'It would indeed,' murmured Alexander.

'How was your journey here? I trust the snow did not cause you any problems?'

'We were fortunate, I fancy, but now we are foisted upon you for several days at least.'

'It is no imposition, I promise you,' replied Marcus. 'No doubt we will be able to find sufficient diversion. With luck we will be able to enjoy my grandfather's *montagne Russe*.'

Isobel sat forward with interest. 'A Russian mountain? What is that?'

'It is a specially built slope, very high and steep at one end, with a long descent that is made in a sleigh that holds four people. My grandfather spent several years in St Petersburg, and discovered these slopes there. He was so taken with them that on his return he had one built here, but unfortunately there is not always sufficient snow for it to be properly employed.'

'It sounds very exciting.'

'It is. We may also be able to demonstrate our skating skills, or lack of them, on the lake. I will have a suitable area cleared of snow.'

Isobel clapped her hands with delight. 'Oh, I do love skating, even if I do keep falling over. I went on the Serpentine
the day before we left London, and I enjoyed it very much
indeed. Aunt Avery was not best pleased with me, as you
may imagine, for she considers skating to be a very unlady-
like pastime, but then she does not approve of many things.
She even frowned a little when the Duke of Devonshire introduced *L'Échange* at his ball.'

'*L'Échange*?' Marcus looked inquiringly at her.

'It's a new cotillion, and has become all the rage in London.
It's a little shocking,' she added, lowering her eyes.

'I am all interest, Lady Isobel,' he replied. 'You must
promise to teach it to me before you leave.'

'I will do so gladly, sir.'

'I look forward to it.'

Her green eyes were speculative. 'Perhaps you will be able
to take it back to America with you,' she murmured.

'Perhaps.'

'You are returning there, aren't you?'

'Have you been lending your ear to below-stairs whisper-
ings, Lady Isobel?'

She flushed a little. 'Yes, I fear so, and so has Elizabeth. Is it
true that you mean to sell Rainworth and then return to
marry an American lady?'

For a moment Elizabeth thought he would not answer, but
then he nodded. 'Shall we just say that there is an element of
truth in the gossip, Lady Isobel?'

'Doesn't your intended bride wish to come here to
England?'

'She has no desire at all to come here.'

'But she will be your duchess, so surely—'

'Both she and her family are staunch supporters of their country's independence, Lady Isobel, and such things as titles do not particularly interest them.'

Elizabeth lowered her glass. 'Are such things of equal uninterest to you, sir?' she asked quietly.

His eyes met hers. 'Why do you ask that?'

'Because by selling Rainworth and then removing to America, you will be effectively bringing the Dukes of Arlingham to an end, will you not?'

'That is a matter for my conscience, Mrs French.'

'That I cannot deny,' she replied, sipping her liqueur again.

A light passed through his eyes, and he looked away from her once more.

Isobel had no intention of allowing the matter to drop. 'What is the lady's name, sir?'

'Miss Constance Bannerman.'

'And where does she reside?'

'Boston.' He turned almost with relief as a footman came to inform them that dinner was now served, and then he quickly offered Isobel his arm. 'Shall we go in, Lady Isobel?'

She accepted, and they preceded Alexander and Elizabeth from the room.

Elizabeth whispered to Alexander. 'He's very cagey about it all, isn't he?'

'That's what I was thinking.'

'I wonder why?'

'The Lord alone knows.'

They dined very handsomely indeed upon roast chicken and a feather-light apricot tart, and Marcus put himself out to be the perfect host. He was full of amusing and witty anecdotes about America, and kept them fully entertained throughout the meal, although Elizabeth could not help but notice that he made no mention at all of Miss Constance Bannerman or her family. She was quite sure that if it had not been for Isobel's direct inquiry, he would not have referred to his bride-to-be at all, which made his interest in Isobel's marital status all that much more curious – troubling even. Why had he asked whether she was married or not, when all the time he was planning to take an American bride? It cannot have been an idle question or Alexander would not have sufficiently remarked upon it to mention the matter to Isobel herself. And then there were the puzzling confusions about which lady actually was Isobel. . . . The more Elizabeth dwelt upon it, the more mystifying it was, especially as Marcus was not paying Isobel any particular attention now, but divided his interest equally between all three guests, except perhaps that he did not speak to Elizabeth herself quite as much as the other two. To Elizabeth he spoke only when spoken to.

After the meal they adjourned to the grand chamber once again, and Isobel lost no time in reminding Marcus that he wished to be taught how to dance *L'Échange*. Pointing out that the new cotillion required two couples, she also drummed Elizabeth and Alexander into dancing as well.

She was an adept teacher, talking Marcus expertly through the figures, and showing him how at the end they changed partners. Oh, how she demonstrated it. With a whirl of her yellow-and-white skirts, she twisted across the floor into Alexander's arms, reaching up to kiss him briefly on the lips before turning brightly back to Marcus again.

'There,' she said, 'is it not a rather shocking measure?'

'Very shocking indeed,' he concurred, his glance sliding a

135

little thoughtfully toward Elizabeth, and then back to Isobel once again. 'I can well imagine that London society's rather jaded appetite finds such a dance very diverting.'

'Oh, yes, there was much flirting and so on at the Devonshire House ball,' replied Isobel, still all innocence.

'Let us go through it all again, so that I may be absolutely sure of everything,' he said, reaching out to take her hand and resume their first position.

Isobel was only too willing to repeat the exercise, and made no demur at all.

Step-by-step they proceeded through the cotillion again, but this time, as Isobel whirled prettily across into Alexander's arms, Marcus stretched out to take Elizabeth's hand, drawing her swiftly into his own embrace, and kissing her on the lips.

He held her close, and for a moment his fingers twined in the warm hair at the nape of her neck, then he released her. 'Keep your wits about you, Mrs French,' he whispered, 'for there is skulduggery afoot, and it is at your expense.'

She stared at him, startled by both the way he had kissed her and the words he had said, but already he had turned away as if nothing had happened. For the remainder of the evening he hardly said anything more to her, and when the ladies elected to retire for the night and leave the gentlemen to spend as long as they liked talking of old times, it was Isobel whom he escorted to her room, giving Elizabeth a courteous but very bland good night.

136

CHAPTER 11

THE SNOW CLOUDS had dispersed the following morning, and
the day dawned upon an England that was completely blan-
keted in white. Few could remember such snow before, and
nearly every lane and highway was blocked, bringing the
entire country to a standstill. Even the sea froze in places, a
phenomenon that was unheard of so far south of the Arctic.
There was nothing anyone could do but endure as best they
could, and it was a prospect that was viewed in entirely opposite ways by the two lady guests at Rainworth Priory.

For Isobel the next few days were, literally, a heaven-sent
opportunity to further her cause with Alexander; for
Elizabeth they were set to be an uncomfortable experience she
would rather have foregone.

She awoke when Violet came in with her customary cup of
morning tea. 'We're snowed in well and truly, madam,' said
the maid, placing the cup and saucer by the bedside and then
going to draw back the curtains.

Elizabeth sat up slowly in the bed. 'Is it very bad?'

'Mr McPherson says he's never known anything like it at
Rainworth before, and he's been here more than fifteen years

137

now. Did you sleep well, madam?'

'Yes. Did you?'

'Oh, yes. What will you wear this morning, madam?'

Elizabeth thought for a moment. 'Did I bring the shell-pink wool with me?'

'Yes, madam.'

'Then I will wear it, and please put out my warmest shawl.'

'Very well, madam.'

Elizabeth finished the tea, and then tossed the bedclothes aside, putting a toe tentatively to the floor. Shivering, she pulled on her wrap, and then stepped into some little slippers before going to the window seat to look out.

There was still ice on the glass, and so once again she breathed upon it and then wiped a little area so that she could see. She found herself gazing upon a white wilderness, where every tree was bowed beneath a burden of snow, and the lake she now knew to be there was detectable only as a vast level area pierced by two tiny treed islands.

Directly in front of the house there was a terrace, the top of its stone balustrade only just visible above the snow. Two Grecian urns marked the place where steps descended into a formal topiary garden where the ornately trimmed shrubs rose like icing-covered pieces on a huge chessboard. Beyond the garden the land dropped again, becoming open parkland as it swept down toward the lake, where she now noticed several boathouses with jetties jutting out from the shore. High above, the sky was a startling blue, and the sunlight was crisp and very clear indeed. The rolling countryside of Sherwood stretched away on all sides, as if into infinity.

She turned from the window, sitting on the seat for a moment with her knees drawn up and clasped in her arms.

She thought of Marcus's enigmatic words the night before. *Keep your wits about you, Mrs French, for there is skulduggery afoot, and it is at your expense.* What on earth had he meant? She had not had an opportunity last night to demand an explanation, but she fully intended to make such an opportunity today.

With a sigh she rose from the window seat, and then went through into the dressing room where Violet was waiting to attend her. About half an hour later, dressed in a high-necked shell-pink woolen gown, and with her hair pinned up into a knot from which fell several bouncy ringlets, she was ready to go down to breakfast, but before she left her room she thought she heard Isobel's laughter coming from outside.

Returning to the window, she saw that it was indeed Isobel. She was squealing with excitement as she bent to gather a snowball and hurl it at Alexander, who was with her in the topiary garden. Evidently some paths had been cleared just out of Elizabeth's view, for Isobel turned to run, unhampered by the deep snow. She looked lovely in a scarlet cloak trimmed with white fur; the cold had stung warm color into her cheeks.

Alexander wore his greatcoat, and he was laughing as well, ducking as the snowball flew past him. He shouted something, apparently mocking Isobel's aim, for she evinced great indignation, and bent to scoop up more snow, which she flung with all her might. This time he was not quick enough to avoid it, and it knocked his hat sideways. Pretending to be furious, he ran toward her, and she squealed again as she fled. They both passed out of Elizabeth's sight, but she could still hear their voices.

Violet had been watching as well. 'Lady Isobel is very

beautiful, isn't she, madam?'

'Yes. Very.'

'It's so sad that she is only here because she has to see her sick father.'

'Yes.' Elizabeth still gazed out of the window at where the others had been a moment before. The thought entered her head that they had seemed extraordinarily happy together, almost as if they were lovers. Her lips parted. Like lovers?

'Shall I show you to the breakfast room, madam?' Violet inquired.

'I . . . I beg your pardon?' Elizabeth was still bemused by her train of thought.

'Shall I show you to the breakfast room?' Violet repeated.

Elizabeth gathered herself. 'Er – no, there is no need. Just tell me where it is.'

'It is off the entrance hall, madam, the door to the right of the dais.'

'Then I am sure to find it,' murmured Elizabeth, glancing out of the window again.

'Is everything all right, madam?'

'Yes, quite all right,' Elizabeth replied more briskly, accepting her shawl and then quickly leaving the room.

Once in the passage she drew the shawl more closely around her shoulders, for it was far colder than in her room. She hurried through the house, pausing only once in the gallery to look down into the cloisters below. There was an enclosed square garden with a stone fountain in the center, and a maid had come from the kitchens to throw crumbs to the hungry birds. As they fluttered gratefully around her, almost taking the food from her fingertips, a black-and-white cat crouched by the wall nearby, his tail flicking angrily to-

and-fro as he watched his prey. The maid finished scattering the crumbs, and then turned to pick up the cross cat and carry him safely back through a doorway into the cloister itself, which had long since been glazed to keep the weather out.

Elizabeth watched the birds for a moment or so more, and then walked quickly on along the gallery. As she descended the grand staircase to the entrance hall, she saw that some of the maids were busy polishing the long table in the center. They turned quickly as they saw her, and bobbed curtsies as they spoke in unison.

'Good morning, madam.'

'Good morning.'

The breakfast room faced the east, and was consequently very bright and sunny on a morning like this. It was also very warm and modern, with a large fire burning in the white marble hearth, and blue-and-white floral wallpaper above white-painted paneling. There was a polished brass fender, and a trivet upon which stood a variety of silver-domed dishes, a bowl of warm bread rolls, and some eggs coddling in a saucepan. A gleaming copper kettle sang softly on its hook directly above the flames.

There was a round table that had been laid with a fresh white cloth. It was set with silver cutlery, blue-and-white porcelain, a silver-gilt coffeepot and a jug of cream, dishes of marmalade, preserves, and honey, and there was a bowl of hothouse carnations in the center. The air was filled with the smell of food, from kedgeree and deviled kidneys, to bacon, sausages, coffee, and, of course, warm bread.

At first she thought there was no one there, but then a figure moved by the brilliantly lit window, and as he stepped out of the light she saw that it was Marcus. He wore a

141

dove-gray coat, cream cord breeches, a maroon brocade waistcoat, and a large unstarched neckcloth that was tied in a complicated knot.

He came to draw out a chair for her. 'Good morning, Mrs French,' he murmured.

The moment she saw him again she was conscious of being affected by everything about him. She wished more and more that it were not so, but as his arm brushed fleetingly against hers, she knew that this man would always have the power to stir her. But it was a power he would never know about, she was resolved upon that, for she was pledged to Alexander, and he was to marry Miss Constance Bannerman. She blushed a little at the path her thoughts were taking, for although she was unwillingly drawn to him, she had no idea at all what he thought of her. Perhaps she was of supreme indifference to him.

He resumed his own seat, evidently having already break-fasted. 'The others could not wait a moment longer before going out in the snow.'

'I know, I saw them from my window.' She remembered her thoughts then, and glanced away.

He noted the glance. 'Did you? Where were they?'

'In the topiary garden.'

'Ah, yes.'

She thought she caught a hint of something in his voice, and looked quickly at him, but at that moment McPherson came in to inquire what she wished to eat.

'Just a little scrambled egg,' she said, when she heard the astonishingly lengthy list. 'And a warm bread roll with some coffee.'

'Madam.'

The butler went to the trivet before the fire, and a moment later her breakfast was placed before her. Then, he withdrew once more.

Marcus studied her. 'Did you sleep well?'

'Very well, thank you.' She wondered how she could broach the matter of his strange remark the night before. Should she just plunge in with a direct question? Or would it be better to lead around to it?

He gave a faint smile. 'I fear that the snow looks set to remain like this for some time, but I am sure we will not be bored.'

'I certainly do not think the others will be,' she replied, the laughter of the snowball fight passing through her thoughts again.

'Why do you say that?'

'They seemed to be enjoying themselves throwing snow-balls.'

'Ah, innocent fun,' he murmured.

'Yes.'

'Is something troubling you, Mrs French?'

She avoided his eyes. 'No, of course not,' she said, beginning to butter her bread roll.

He continued to look at her for a moment, but then stretched across the table to drop her earrings on to the cloth by her plate. 'Yours, I believe,' he said softly.

She gazed gladly at them. 'Oh, thank you so much for retrieving them, I'm truly grateful.'

'Then I am delighted to have been of assistance.'

She raised her eyes a little guiltily. 'I still feel wretched for having fled from the lane like that.'

'It was thoughtless of me to request you to wait. If I had

had any sense I would have asked for your name and address, so please do not blame yourself.' He smiled.

Her heart almost turned over, for it was a warm smile, almost caressing. No, she was letting her imagination run away with her again. It was just a smile, and to see anything else in it was to be guilty of wishful thinking on the part of her treacherous emotions. She felt telltale color stain her cheeks again, and quickly she began to eat her breakfast.

'Does Lady Isobel have a particular suitor, Mrs French?' he asked suddenly.

She lowered her knife and fork. 'Why do you wish to know?'

'Idle curiosity.'

'I do not think that is so, sir.'

'I'm of a mind to be offended by your lack of belief,' he murmured, pouring himself another cup of coffee.

'I gather that you have shown a more than passing interest in my cousin, and so I am naturally equally as interested in your reasons, for Isobel is actually in my care at the moment.'

'Oh, believe me, Mrs French, I have not been displaying any out-of-the-ordinary interest in Lady Isobel. I apologize if that is the impression I have managed to convey.'

She was a little nonplussed, for only a moment or so before he had asked point-blank if Isobel had a particular suitor. 'Well, sir, it is the impression you have managed to convey, and since you are not at liberty to consider a bride here in England when you are about to take one in America, I am sure you will understand my concern.'

The ghost of a smile played on his lips. 'There are very few of us who are at liberty to do as we please, Mrs French.'

'But some of us are apparently at liberty to utter enigmatic statements without troubling to explain what they've said,' she replied, suddenly deciding to confront him about what he'd said the night before. 'What did you mean about there being skulduggery afoot?'

'Ah, well, perhaps I enjoyed a glass or two too much wine on that occasion.'

'You were very far from being in your cups, sir. Please do me the courtesy of explaining.'

'It was a spur-of-the-moment remark, Mrs French, and maybe I was wrong to say anything at all, for to be sure it is none of my business.'

'You made it your business, my lord duke.'

'Yes, I know, and now I do not think it was the right thing to do.'

'I mean to get to the bottom of it, sir, and I will be irritatingly persistent until you give in.'

'I would prefer not to interfere, Mrs French.'

'You already have, it seems,' she said. 'Please, sir, tell me what is on your mind.'

He sat back in his chair, his fingers drumming on the table for a moment, and then he met her eyes. 'Very well, if you insist. There is indeed skulduggery afoot, and it is being instigated by Lady Isobel. I believe that she is in love with Alexander, and from my own observations I would say that he is not making much of an effort to spurn her advances.'

She stared at him. She could hear Isobel's laughter, and see Alexander's face as he gave chase in the snowy garden.

Marcus watched her. 'Last night I was certain that you had not guessed, but now. . . . Have you noticed for yourself?'

'No.'

'Mrs French—'

'No! You are wrong.'

'I wish I were, but I am not a fool. I observed Lady Isobel last night, and she gave herself away on every occasion. Each time she glanced at him, she—'

'You are wrong,' Elizabeth repeated, pushing her plate away, her appetite gone.

'I did not want to tell you, and last night I merely wished to put you on your mettle, to make you think a little. I could not believe that you hadn't detected it all yourself, for you are a very intelligent woman, and far from a green girl. But your head appeared to be in the clouds, and you seemed unaware of everything.'

'Perhaps because there has not been anything of which I should be aware,' she replied, but in her heart of hearts she knew it was true. She wished everything could be as it had been before she had gone to Hanover Square. That was when it had all begun to go sadly wrong, and now nothing was the same anymore.

'Your assertion is not very convincing, Mrs French, for it is clear to me that something has happened to make you begin to realize for yourself what has been going on under your nose.'

She wanted to bring the painful conversation to a close, and so she rose to her feet, tossing her napkin on to the table. 'Do you always treat your guests in this way, sir?' she asked, her voice trembling even though she tried to keep it level.

He got up as well, leaning his hands on the table as he looked earnestly at her. 'Not to have said anything at all would have been to do you a grave disservice, and I think far too highly of you to do that. I didn't know what to say exactly, but I hoped that my remark about skulduggery might at least make you look around with open eyes. I wanted you to see it all for yourself, without any interference from me, but you demanded a full explanation. I would not insult you by inventing some tale to fob you off, and when I realized that nothing would do but that I told you, I replied in all honesty. I do indeed believe that Lady Isobel has fallen in love with Alexander, and that she may succeed in winning him unless you do something about it. If you want to keep him, then you will do it easily, for beautiful and charming as she may be, she cannot hold a candle to you, Elizabeth.'

She looked quickly at him. 'I gave you no leave to address me by my first name.'

'Then I have presumed, forgive me.'

'I trust that not a word of this conversation will pass your lips, sir.'

'Do you really imagine that I would repeat any of this elsewhere?'

'I don't know what to think where you are concerned, my lord duke.'

'I have not dealt dishonestly with you, I assure you.'

She didn't reply.

'What do you intend to do?' he asked after a moment.

'That is my concern, sir.'

He nodded. 'Yes, it is. Forgive me again.' He drew a long breath, and tactfully changed the subject. 'I promised the others that we would follow them on their walk. Do you wish to do that?'

'Yes.'

'My man will have brought my outdoor garments to the hall by now, for I told him some time ago of my intentions, but if you wish to go to your room to change. . . ?' He glanced

147

at her breakfast, which was now congealing upon the plate.

'I will go now,' she said, gathering her skirts and escaping gladly from the room.

She was close to tears as she hastened back up the staircase, and she paused again in the gallery in order to compose herself before facing Violet, who would still be in her room.

Looking down into the cloister garden again, she saw that the birds had gone now, leaving countless tiny prints upon the snow. She pressed her hot forehead to the ice-cold glass, and closed her eyes for a moment.

Isobel was in love with Alexander, it was a fact that she could not deny. It had been there in her cousin's animated face as she'd laughed with him in the garden earlier on. There were other clues too. At the Devonshire House ball Isobel had undergone a virtual metamorphosis, suddenly becoming all that was friendly and warm. Why? Because she had seen Alexander. That same night she had inveigled her way into their carriage, and had thus managed to be close to him for a little longer. Then there had been the exhibition at Ackermann's, the fainting spell in Hyde Park, and now the journey up here to Nottinghamshire. It all fell into place, as did her endless sparkling conversation in the carriage. As for Alexander. . . .

With a sigh, Elizabeth opened her eyes again, staring down into the snow-covered garden below. What did he feel? Had she, by her own contrary behavior recently, virtually driven him into Isobel's arms? She remembered how angry he had been over her withdrawn moods, and then how indulgent with Isobel, even to tolerating her chatter about *Childe Harold's Pilgrimage*. Yes, he had a great deal of time for Isobel, a great deal of time indeed, but was he turning to her?

'Madam?'

Violet spoke behind her, and with a gasp Elizabeth whirled about.

The maid looked at her with great concern. 'Are you all right, madam?'

'I . . . I have a slight headache, that's all. I am on my way back to my room to change to go out, for the duke and I are to take a walk together. I am sure the fresh air will clear my head.'

'Which clothes do you wish to wear, madam? I will hurry straight back to put them out for you.'

'You choose, Violet, for I do not mind.'

'Madam.' Bobbing a curtsy, the maid hurried away again.

Elizabeth followed slowly in her wake, her thoughts still upon Isobel and Alexander. What should she do about it all? She could hardly say anything to Isobel, for that would not be appropriate. Perhaps she should face Alexander? Yes, that was what she must do. At the first opportunity, she must speak privately with him.

CHAPTER 12

ISOBEL'S EXCITED SQUEALS of laughter rang out over the frozen lake as she and Alexander endeavored to skate on the area of ice that had been cleared of snow. She wobbled and slithered, her wooden skates threatening all the while to slip away from under her, and to prevent herself from falling she clung very tightly indeed to Alexander's hand. His other arm was protectively around her tiny waist. Her scarlet cloak was a brilliant splash of warm color against the surrounding hues of winter, and her face was flushed with happiness as she smiled up into his face, and clung more tightly still as her skates wobbled alarmingly again.

Elizabeth was seated nearby on an upturned rowing boat in the lee of one of the boathouses. She wore her aquamarine cloak, and her cold hands were thrust deep into a muff. Her thoughtful eyes followed Isobel's noisy progress over the ice, for everything that young lady did now was of immense interest. Just how much truth was there in what Marcus had said? And in what she herself had begun to suspect anyway?

Behind the boathouses, Rainworth faced grandly over its snow-covered park, several of its churchlike windows shining brightly in the cold January sunlight. The brittle air echoed with the scrape of shovels as several teams of men strove to clear as many paths as possible, and other men were shaking snow from the overladen branches of evergreen trees, some of which were bowed alarmingly low beneath the unaccustomed weight. Horses whinnied and stamped in the stables, and a dog barked constantly somewhere nearby. Pheasants could be heard calling harshly in the trees edging the lake, and a flight of wild ducks skimmed low over the frozen surface, too afraid of the deep snow to attempt to land. A small herd of red deer had ventured from the surrounding woodland, tempted closer to the house by the knowledge that soon their hunger would be satisfied by the provision of hay from one of the barns.

Elizabeth continued to watch Isobel, whose smiles and clinging manner were a little too obvious for comfort, although it could not with absolute honesty be said that her conduct so far had actually progressed beyond the bounds of propriety. It was nevertheless clear to Elizabeth that Isobel was indeed in love with Alexander, but his feelings were impossible to gauge with any certainty. Perhaps he was simply humoring her; perhaps it was much, much more.

Elizabeth glanced at Marcus as he stood about six feet away from her on part of the jetty that had been scraped clear of snow. He had not mentioned their breakfast conversation again, and his manner had been all that was correct and courteous from the moment she had rejoined him to come outside. But as he watched the two skaters now, he could only be thinking of what he had said of them.

There was a natural grace about him as he stood with one boot resting on a wooden mooring post. The cut of his clothes was impeccable, from the clinging lines of his breeches, to the elegant fullness of his gray greatcoat. The brim of his tall-crowned hat cast a shadow over his face, but she could still see the blue of his eyes as they followed Isobel and Alexander upon the ice. His profile was flawless and his blond hair very pale against the black beaver of his hat.

On the ice, Isobel finally lost her balance completely, and this time she brought Alexander tumbling down with her. They collapsed in a heap on the ice, both of them quite helpless with laughter.

Marcus turned, his gaze penetrating as he looked directly at Elizabeth. He did not say anything as their eyes met, and it was she who looked away first.

He straightened then, calling out to the others. 'I think it is time we called a halt and went inside, don't you?'

Alexander was helping Isobel to her feet. 'As you wish,' he called back.

Isobel was dismayed. 'Oh, no, let's stay a little longer. It's so much fun.'

'Mrs French and I are slowly freezing to the ground.'

'Then you go back, or better still, join us on the ice!' suggested Isobel hopefully, still holding on to Alexander because she was unsteady on her skates.

Marcus shook his head. 'I think we should all go back, for we've been out in this cold long enough for a first time, and besides, I've instructed McPherson to have some good hot bishop prepared. It will be waiting for us by the fire in the grand chamber.'

Isobel hesitated, for she adored a glass of bishop, with its delicious flavor of roasted oranges, cloves, ginger, and port wine. Tottering to the side of the lake, she leaned on

Alexander's arm as she made her unsteady way to Elizabeth's boat, where she sat down to take off her skates.

When they were all ready to walk back to the house, Elizabeth anticipated her cousin by stepping over swiftly to take Alexander's arm first. A brief spark of irritation flashed in Isobel's green eyes, but she had no option but to take Marcus's arm instead.

Marcus read Elizabeth's action accurately, and as their glance met briefly, a faint smile played upon his lips. Then he led Isobel toward the path first, leaving Elizabeth free to dawdle with Alexander if she wished, and thus take any opportunity that arose for setting about whatever purpose she had decided upon.

Elizabeth did indeed dawdle, for she did not know quite what to say. Alexander had not appeared to notice anything amiss when she had so deliberately stepped in before Isobel, and the moment her hand was on his arm, he had placed his own tenderly over it. He smiled into her eyes, and seemed to be as loving and warm as he had been before she herself had begun to spoil everything. Did it mean that Isobel's was an unrequited love?

At last she braced herself to say something. 'Isobel enjoyed herself a great deal on the skates, didn't she?'

'Oh, yes. It is so refreshing to see someone making her pleasure so plain. She is entirely without artifice, and I find her very charming.'

'Yes, I know.'

He glanced at her, for she had spoken in an oddly quiet tone. 'Is something wrong?'

'I feel I must talk to you about Isobel, Alexander,' she replied, watching Isobel's dainty scarlet-clad figure as she

153

and Marcus drew farther and farther ahead.

Alexander halted. 'Talk to me about her? Whatever for?'

She found it difficult to meet his eyes. 'Alexander, I think that Isobel is in love with you, and—'

'In love with me?' he interrupted incredulously. 'But that's nonsense!'

'Is it? Forgive me, Alexander, but I fear I have to disagree. I cannot help but notice how she is when she is with you, and I have to say that I wish . . .'

'Yes?' His hazel eyes were a little cool.

'I have to say that it would be better if you were a little less encouraging where she is concerned.'

'Encouraging? I am merely being as agreeable toward her as she is to me. I must say, Elizabeth, I find your comments almost offensive.' He had drawn away from her, and everything about him was suddenly stiff.

Elizabeth colored a little. 'I do not mean to be offensive, but it isn't a very easy subject to bring up.'

'It should not have been brought up at all,' he replied in a clipped tone.

She bridled a little. 'It *had* to be brought up, for I refuse to stand idly by and watch my own cousin endeavoring to usurp me.'

'You are wrong about her, I assure you.'

'Am I? Alexander, she has managed to find her way into your company far too frequently for it to be mere coincidence. First there was the night of the ball, then Ackermann's, then Hyde Park, and now this journey, during which she has positively hogged your attention!'

He became angry at that. 'I am gravely disappointed in you, Elizabeth, for your cousin is under a great deal of stress

154

at the moment, and is doing her level best to hide her unhappiness by being cheerful and bright, and all you can do is
accuse her of trying to win me!'

'Doing her best to hide her unhappiness?' Elizabeth was
almost speechless. 'Is that how you see her conduct?
Alexander, I doubt very much if she has given her father a
great deal of thought over the past few days, indeed I am
beginning to suspect that he is by no means as ill as we have
been led to believe.'

'What a monstrous thing to say,' he breathed. 'Elizabeth, I
would never have believed you capable of such unkindness,
indeed you begin to appear heartless in the extreme!'

She controlled her fury. 'If I am heartless, sir, then you are
either very foolish or very sly. At the moment I am not quite
sure which it is.'

'Foolish? Sly? I think you had best explain exactly what you
mean, madam!' he snapped.

'Very well. If you are foolish, it is because you are permitting Isobel many liberties which she can only find inviting
and encouraging. If you are sly, it is because you know full
well what is going on, and you are enjoying her attentions. Is
that the truth of it, Alexander? Is she flattering your vanity,
and are you basking in it all?'

'I will not dignify your base charges with an answer,' he
replied coldly.

'Why? Because an honest response would show you in a
shabby light?'

'So now I am shabby as well, am I?'

'I have to wonder how you would have conducted yourself
if it had been Isobel who accompanied you back to the house
now. Would you have smiled into her eyes as you smiled into

mine? Would you have placed your hand as tenderly over hers as you placed it over mine? I begin to think that you would.'

A nerve flickered at the corner of his mouth. 'Perhaps you find it possible to think such things of me because your own behavior has been somewhat shabby of late.'

'*My* behavior? Oh, I may have been a little quiet and reserved, but it cannot be compared with you—'

'It is your reason for being quiet and withdrawn that is of concern, Elizabeth,' he interrupted. 'You have managed to convey to me that I cannot possibly match up to the ideal that was once your precious James. Oh, he may have become a monster, but in the beginning he was everything to you, everything that I am not and never will be. There is very little pleasure and reward in always being second best, but that is apparently the role you have allotted to me.'

'That is not true!' she cried, a flood of hot color rushing into her cheeks.

'No?'

'No!' But guilt washed through her.

'Forgive me if I take your reassurance with a pinch of salt, madam, for I do not only have my own observations to judge by.'

She searched his face. 'Then who else's as well?' she demanded.

He was on the point of telling her, but then thought better of it, and looked away in silence.

She continued to search his face, and then realized who this other source must be. 'Isobel? Is it Isobel?'

Still he did not reply, but now his silence was eloquent.

'So, it *is* Isobel! How very coincidental. It would suit her purposes very well to sow such a seed of doubt, would it not?'

'Are you now going to accuse her of telling lies?'

'I am accusing her of an ulterior motive, sir,' she replied angrily. Oh, this was going from bad to worse. She wished she could turn the clock back and begin again, but it was too late now, and harsh accusations had been made on both sides.

He removed his hat to run his fingers slowly through his hair, as if to take a moment or so to think clearly. 'Perhaps we should postpone the betrothal, Elizabeth, for it is plain that things are very far from right between us.'

She swallowed, for tears were pricking her eyes and she felt a sob rise in her throat. 'Do ... do you wish to withdraw entirely from the match?' she asked, unable to prevent her voice from catching.

'I merely think it would be better to delay until we have sorted all this out. I deny that Isobel is in love with me, and I also deny that I have been guilty of encouraging her. You deny that you compare me with what you lost with James. We are both angry and in no mood to be reasonable, so I suggest we leave the matter for the time being.'

'As you wish.'

He offered her his arm again, and hesitantly she accepted. This time he did not put his hand over hers, and she did not move close to him. Their steps crunched on the remnants of the snow on the path, and that was the only sound they made. Not a word was uttered, not a glance exchanged.

She felt wretched, and more guilty than he could possibly know, for if the truth were known she also had Marcus Sheridan on her conscience. It was no longer over James alone that she should be accused, but over the handsome master of

Rainworth as well.

The others had now vanished into the house to enjoy the drink of bishop that awaited them, and as Elizabeth and Alexander entered the hall, she felt she could not face them just yet. Alexander's prickly coldness would be evident, Isobel was bound to pick up such strong undercurrents, and Marcus would guess that her conversation with Alexander had become a bitter confrontation. It would be better to avoid any further embarrassment for the time being.

She turned to Alexander. 'I . . . I think I will forgo the bishop,' she said quietly.

'Elizabeth, I do not intend to make things difficult.'

'No. I do not for a moment think you do, it is just that I would prefer to go to my room for a while. Please make my excuses to the others. Tell them I have a headache.'

'Very well.'

He watched as she went quickly up the staircase, and then he turned, for McPherson had appeared to relieve him of his outdoor garments.

'His Grace and Lady Isobel are already in the grand chamber, Sir Alexander,' the butler said.

'Thank you, McPherson.' Toying with his cuff for a moment, Alexander glanced again at the staircase where Elizabeth had gone, then he walked toward the door of the grand chamber.

Isobel was seated by the fire, where she had sat the night before, and she lowered her glass of bishop as he entered. 'Ah, there you are. . . . Where is Elizabeth?'

'She – er – has a slight headache, and has gone to rest for a while,' he replied, avoiding her eyes as he went to take a seat.

Marcus bent to ladle some of the bishop out of the bowl on

the hearth into another glass, which he gave to Alexander. 'I trust she is not too indisposed?' he inquired lightly.

'Er – no – I don't think so.'

Marcus said no more, but his eyes were pensive.

Elizabeth did not go directly to her room, but paused once more at her place in the gallery in order to be certain of being fully composed when she saw Violet. The cloister garden was deserted, except for a magpie perched on top of the stone fountain. As she watched, the bird flew away in alarm, startled by the ever-watchful cat. In a moment the peaceful scene below had been shattered, just as the peace and tranquility of her own life had been shattered.

With a heavy heart she turned to walk on, but as she did so she noticed that one of the doors off the gallery stood ajar, and she could see that the room beyond was a magnificent galleried library. On impulse she went inside.

It was a truly beautiful room, with glass-fronted cabinets stretching from the floor up to the wooden gallery, and then encircling the gallery as well. The doors of these cabinets were shaped like church windows, with trefoils and tracery, and the volumes on the shelves were gilded and leatherbound. A low fire glowed in the hearth, indicating that it was a room that Marcus intended to use, and in the center of the floor there was an immense writing desk with a comfortable chair. Everything required for writing letters stood upon the desk's green leather surface, from an elegant silver-gilt pen stand with a crystal bottle for the ink, to a handsome ivory-handled blotter and a candlestick that was solely for the purpose of melting sealing wax.

She glanced appreciatively around, for she had seldom

seen such a well-stocked and agreeable library. Then her attention was drawn back to the writing desk, for there was another item upon it which she had not noticed at first. It was an oval miniature of a beautiful young woman, and was set in a golden frame. The young woman had tumbling honey-colored curls and laughing brown eyes, and she wore a magnolia silk gown that revealed her slender but curvaceous figure. There were roses in her hair, and in the graceful wicker basket she held, and behind her there was a white-pillared house set in a fine but vaguely foreign-looking park.

Curious, Elizabeth went to pick up the little portrait. At first there did not seem to be any indication as to who the lady might be, but as she turned the frame over she saw an engraved nameplate on the back. *Miss Constance Bannerman. Boston. 1812.*

So this was the lady Marcus was returning to America to marry. Elizabeth gazed at the lovely painted face. Constance Bannerman was radiantly beautiful, and it was easy to see why she had captured the heart of a man like Marcus.

Slowly she replaced the miniature, and then turned to leave. Her footsteps echoed along the quiet gallery, a sound as empty and lonely as her heart.

CHAPTER 13

IT WAS EARLY afternoon, and Elizabeth was seated in the window of her room trying to summon the courage to rejoin the others. She felt low and dispirited, and would have liked to have taken further refuge in her invented headache in order to hide away where she was, but she knew that that would only be to postpone the inevitable. Some time or other she had to face her companions, and the longer she tried to put it off, the worse it would be.

She was just steeling herself to rejoin them when there was a knock at her door, and Violet went to see who it was. Marcus stood there, and Elizabeth heard him ask if he could see her.

The maid turned inquiringly, not sure whether her mistress wished to receive him or not, but Elizabeth nodded. 'That's all right, Violet, please show His Grace in.'

Violet bobbed a curtsy, and stood politely aside for him to enter.

The sunlight from the window shone brightly on his hair as he came toward her, and her hand trembled a little as he raised it to his lips.

'Your Grace?' she murmured, drawing her fingers slowly but firmly away because she was already conscious of a slight blush warming her cheeks.

'I trust you are feeling a little better now?'

'Er – yes. Yes, I am.'

'I'm so glad to hear it. Forgive me for coming to you like this, but my purpose is twofold.'

'Twofold?'

'First, I must return these yet again.' He took something from his pocket and held his hand out to her, dropping her earrings into her palm. 'You left them on the breakfast table. I meant to return them earlier, but they slipped my mind.'

'I . . . I will endeavor to look after them properly from now on,' she said, feeling a little foolish. Then she met his eyes again. 'You said your purpose was twofold?'

'Yes. I am also here to persuade you to join us in a while when we sally forth to the *montagne Russe*. It is ready to be used now, and is really best enjoyed by four people, for it is with four that the sleigh is properly balanced. I sincerely hope that you feel up to indulging a little.'

Her resolve faltered. 'Perhaps my presence will be a dampener . . .'

'I doubt that very much.' He smiled a little. 'Maybe I have no right to say anything, but I think that under the circumstances it would be better if you could take the bull by the proverbial horns, for to delay will not achieve anything except to make you feel worse.'

Her face felt dreadfully hot, and she couldn't meet his eyes. 'You are disconcertingly perceptive, sir,' she murmured.

'Where you are concerned, perhaps.' Briefly, oh, so briefly, his hand touched her cheek.

Her gaze flew to his. Where she was concerned?

But he did not explain. 'Join us, Mrs French, and be assured that an excellent time will be had by all. We leave in half an hour, and will await you in the hall.'

Without waiting for her to reply, he bowed and left.

Elizabeth remained where she was, gazing at the door as it closed behind him. She felt as if he understood her more than Alexander ever had, and it was a strange sensation. She hardly knew him, and yet he had invaded her dreams and her daylight hours in a way that scarcely seemed credible. Constance Bannerman was a very fortunate woman. . . .

Shortly afterwards, Elizabeth did indeed take the bull by the horns, and went down to join the others in the hall. She wore her aquamarine cloak and overshoes, and her hood was raised over her hair. Her hands were warm in her muff, and she had put a little rouge on her cheeks in the hope of looking less strained and tense than she felt.

Isobel was again wearing her scarlet cloak, and was seated on one of the chairs arranged around the long table in the center of the floor. Evidently there was something wrong with one of her overshoes, for Alexander was crouching before her, retying the long laces.

Marcus saw Elizabeth first, and came to meet her at the foot of the staircase. 'I am so glad that you are able to join us, Mrs French,' he said, holding his hand out to her.

Hearing this, Alexander rose swiftly to his feet, looking directly toward her. She felt his gaze upon her, but did not meet it. Even now, after all that had been said, he was dancing attendance upon Isobel, and by getting to his feet so sharply and almost guiltily, he had revealed to her that he

163

knew full well he was at fault.

Isobel's quick green glance moved from Alexander to Elizabeth, and then back to Alexander again, for with her vested interest in how things were between them, she knew that they had had a serious difference. But what about? Whatever it was, they were decidedly cool toward one another, with neither of them displaying any intention of making the first move toward reconciliation.

McPherson came to tell them that the sleigh was waiting outside. Isobel immediately took Alexander's arm. 'Oh, isn't this exciting?' she breathed, her eyes shining. 'I'm looking forward to it so much that I cannot recall when last I felt like this. I believe I must have been about eight or nine, for it really is very childish of me.' She smiled up into his eyes, clinging to his arm as animatedly as if she were anticipating a wonderful treat, but really she was using the moment as an excuse to press home the difference between her and her withdrawn, rather cool cousin. I am fun to be with, she was telling him, whereas Elizabeth is not only very dull but also very difficult. She was rewarded by his quick return of the smile, and by the way he squeezed his arm, the brief pressure detected by her, but invisible to the others.

Marcus had already drawn Elizabeth's hand over his sleeve. He said nothing, but led her firmly toward the door, and then out into the frostbitten afternoon, where the sun had not made any impression at all upon the snow.

The sleigh was very striking; at the front it was shaped like a swan with half-raised wings that protected the seats inside. There was a golden crown on the swan's head, and the whole sleigh was painted white with lavish gilding everywhere. The seats were rather oddly arranged in single file, the front one low, the second higher, the third low again, and the one at the back again higher, but it soon became clear why they were placed like that, for Marcus explained that the lower seats were for the ladies, and that the gentlemen were to sit on the higher ones, protecting the lady in front with their arms.

The sleigh was drawn by two horses that would pull it across the park to the ice mountain, where they would be unharnessed and then the sleigh dragged up the slope by a team of men who were waiting in readiness. Then, with its four passengers safely ensconced, it would slide down the long slope at great speed, coming to a halt only when it reached a specially built uphill gradient that would put a natural brake upon its momentum.

As soon as Marcus had finished explaining about the sleigh's seating, Isobel acted quickly to deny Alexander any opportunity he may have sought to sit with Elizabeth. Taking his hand, she climbed quickly into the front seat, turning her green eyes pleadingly upon him as she did so. 'You will hold me tight when we go down the mountain, won't you?'

'Yes, of course,' he replied, assisting her to sit down comfortably, and then getting into the high seat immediately behind her.

Elizabeth's resolve faltered again as she watched them, and she felt deeply hurt that Alexander could so easily ignore her feelings. Was his anger with her sufficient justification for this?

Marcus suddenly placed himself in front of her, so that she could not see the others. 'Allow me to help you into your seat, Mrs French,' he said gently, leading her forward before she could somehow cry off.

Reluctantly she permitted him to help her into the third

seat, behind Alexander. There were tears in her eyes, but she blinked them fiercely away. She wouldn't break down here in front of everyone, she wouldn't!

Marcus climbed into the seat behind, and slipped his arms gently around her, then nodded to the stableboy who was to lead the horses across the park. As soon as the sleigh began to slide forward, bells on the horses' harness jingled in time to their action. The boy ran as he led them along a wide cleared pathway, and the sleigh's runners whined over the layer of hard snow that had been left.

The *montagne Russe* filled a sloping clearing in a small woodland of pine trees. The clearing was evidently very ancient indeed, for it was edged by the distinctive mounds of prehistoric earthworks. Apart from the tall pine trees, there were many holly bushes, their branches brilliant with scarlet berries that were the same color as Isobel's cloak, but it was the ice mountain that dominated the surroundings. It rose sharply at the higher end of the clearing, so sharply that its summit could only be reached by climbing a long flight of wooden steps with a handrail. From a flat platform at the top, the slope itself swooped down toward the far end of the clearing, where the special uphill gradient Marcus had mentioned could be clearly seen among the trees. From the platform to the end of the slope was about one hundred and fifty yards in length, and it was clear that the sleigh would descend very swiftly indeed.

Isobel's eyes widened as the sleigh halted and the boy began to unharness the horses. She gazed up at the towering slope, and then looked at Marcus. 'Are we really going to descend that?'

'We are, Lady Isobel.'

166

'But it's huge!'

'There would be little point in making it small,' he replied with a smile, getting out and assisting Elizabeth.

Isobel put her little hand in Alexander's, managing to stumble prettily as she alighted, thus giving herself another opportunity to cling to him for a moment. She knew she was being entirely shameless now, taking liberties right in front of Elizabeth, but she simply couldn't help herself. Her feelings for Alexander had run away with her, and sometimes she was within a heartbeat of putting her arms around him and kissing him. She wanted to force the issue now because she was carried away by the hope that the differences between Elizabeth and him were irreconcilable. She knew that he liked her, and responded to her, and if only she knew once and for all that he no longer loved Elizabeth, then everything would be so simple. . . .

The men who had been waiting for the sleigh's arrival now came over to drag it up the slope, and the boy led the horses to the side of the clearing, where some blankets had been put to place over them until they were required to take the sleigh back to the house again.

Still claiming Alexander's attention entirely for herself, Isobel began to climb up the steep wooden steps. She held on tightly to the handrail, and was all aflutter when from time to time she glanced back down and saw how high she was.

Elizabeth stood in the snow watching them, and she gave a start when Marcus spoke close to her. 'Shall we go up as well, Mrs French?'

'Yes, I suppose so.'

'Have you so little enthusiasm?' he inquired.

She continued to look at the others. 'How would you be

167

feeling if you were me?' she asked in return.

He was silent for a moment. 'Perhaps I would be analyzing my reactions,' he said at last.

She looked quickly at him. 'And what conclusion would you reach?'

'That I was perhaps not in love with my official partner after all.'

She stared at him. 'Is that really what you think?'

'Yes,' he replied frankly. 'Mrs French, if you loved Alexander, you would have shed more tears than this. Oh, you are shaken, there is no mistaking that, but you are not heartbroken, are you?' He looked deep into her eyes. 'There is much more to this than at first meets the eye, but I am not yet quite sure what it is. I cannot for a moment imagine that you have been unfaithful to him, but if you had, then that might explain your conduct.'

'You go too far, sir,' she replied shortly, turning away from him.

'Maybe I do, Mrs French, but you did ask me what conclusion I would reach,' he pointed out.

'Then I will tell you that I have most certainly not been unfaithful to Alexander, or to anyone else.' She glanced toward the steps. 'I think it is time we joined the others, don't you?' she said, beginning to ascend them.

He remained close behind her throughout the long ascent, catching her arm only once when her overshoe slipped on some ice. They reached the top to find the others ready and waiting in the sleigh, which was being held at the head of the slope by ropes that would be released to allow it to make the swooping descent, the end of which seemed an alarmingly long distance away.

Marcus took her hand to help her into the third seat, and then he resumed his place behind her, placing his arms protectively around her in readiness. His lips were close to her ear as he whispered.

'Maybe you have been all that is actually faithful, Elizabeth, but in your thoughts you have strayed, haven't you?'

Her breath caught, and her heartbeats quickened guiltily, but then he nodded at the waiting men, who immediately released the ropes.

Isobel squealed as the sleigh leaped forward and began to gather speed down the long incline. Her hood was blown back from her head, and her chestnut hair tugged at its pins. The air was bitterly cold against her face, and the sleigh's runners whined over the ice.

Elizabeth's hood was blown back as well, and her hair was less well behaved. Several unruly curls fell free from their pins, and her stomach lurched as the sleigh made the wild descent. She pressed back involuntarily against Marcus, her trembling hands clinging to his arms, and as the tree trunks and holly bushes seemed to hurl themselves toward her, she had to close her eyes to shut everything out.

At last the sleigh's headlong flight was checked, and the whining of its runners became a mere whisper as it slid to a halt and then fell slowly back down the little gradient at the end.

Isobel's eyes were bright with excitement, and she gave a half-laugh. 'I . . . I don't know whether to say I enjoyed it or I was terrified by it,' she declared.

Marcus alighted. 'The truth will come from your response to my next question, Lady Isobel. Do you wish to do it again?'

She smiled impishly at him. 'Oh, yes, please.'

'Then you enjoyed it well enough.' He turned to Elizabeth. 'And what of you, Mrs French? Does the *montagne Russe* meet with your approval?'

She thought of how she'd pressed back into his arms, and of how good it had felt. 'Yes, sir, it meets with my approval,' she replied. He had told her that she should analyze her reactions, and that was precisely what she had done during those breathless moments of the descent. She had enjoyed being so close to him, enjoyed more than she should the intimacy of having his arms around her, and she had done so because she was moving even closer to falling in love with him.

It had begun in Hanover Square, before she had even known who he was, and it had increased with each subsequent meeting. He was right to tell her that she did not truly love Alexander, for she had herself realized that she felt only a very deep affection for the man she had pledged to marry, but Marcus Sheridan had no right at all to conduct himself toward her as he did. Oh, he had not taken any physical liberties, but verbally he had made a number of advances that went beyond those of a mere friend. Even if he believed that her liaison with Alexander was coming to an end, he was himself far from free to act, for Miss Constance Bannerman awaited him in America. If it was simply seduction that he had in mind, a casual dalliance to amuse himself with while he was in England, then he was guilty of a grave misjudgment. Elizabeth French would never indulge in such an *amour*, for she had suffered the humiliation of being betrayed, and so would never dream of consigning the absent Miss Bannerman to such hurt. And apart from that, she, Elizabeth, valued herself too highly to stoop to idle liaisons.

As Marcus assisted her from the sleigh, she hoped that she was wrong about him, and that something as disreputable as seduction was far from his thoughts. She did not know him well, and perhaps was simply misreading his manner. She was far from composed at the moment, and was probably too unsettled to be truly sensible on such a matter.

They returned to the other end of the ice mountain, and as they climbed the wooden steps once more, the team of men dragged the sleigh back to the platform at the top of the slope. The second descent wasn't quite as nerve-wracking as the first, and by the time they made a third, both Isobel and Elizabeth had begun to find it very exhilarating.

They had been enjoying the diversion for nearly an hour when Marcus thought there was something wrong with one of the sleigh's runners, making it unsafe for hazardous descents of the mountain, but safe to return to the house, and as he and Alexander examined it closely in order to be sure that it was safe, Elizabeth and Isobel adjourned to one of the holly-covered mounds at the edge of the clearing.

The examination of the sleigh took longer than expected, and Isobel began to fidget. She glanced around, pouting a little as she wished the men would hurry so that they could all make another descent. She looked at the tangled holly bushes nearby, and her attention was drawn to one particular cluster of berries. She tried to count them, and knew that there were at least a dozen, all formed into a perfect ball with two dark green leaves emerging beneath them. She thought how pretty they looked, and how much to advantage they would appear on her muff, for the berries were the very same color as her cloak. Glancing back at the sleigh, she saw that Alexander and Marcus were still deep in examination, and so

171

she stepped through the snow toward the holly spray. It was higher than she realized, and she had to stretch up to reach it.

At that moment a flock of jackdaws rose from the trees nearby, startled by something farther in the woods. The noise distracted Isobel for a fleeting second, and she lost her balance. The ground dipped sharply away beyond the holly bush, the drop concealed by the spread of the branches, and the clamor of the jackdaws drowned her brief cry as she fell. Then she struck her head on a branch and lost consciousness as she tumbled down through the snow to the foot of the mound.

Elizabeth knew nothing of what had happened, for her attention was on the men by the sleigh, and with the cries of the excited birds echoing all around she did not hear anything else. It wasn't until something made her turn to say something to her cousin that she knew anything had happened.

'Isobel?' She glanced around in puzzlement. Then she saw the marks in the snow, and the slight scattering of broken holly leaves that told of a fall. 'Isobel?' she said again, stepping tentatively toward the disturbed snow.

There was no answer, and Elizabeth began to feel alarmed. The clamor of the birds died away into silence. 'Isobel?' she called, glancing around again.

Hearing, Marcus and Alexander straightened and looked toward her.

She continued to cast anxiously around, but Isobel seemed to have vanished. Then she looked down through the tangle of holly, and saw a splash of scarlet against the snow at the foot of the mound. With a dismayed gasp, she scrambled down, hardly noticing the sharp leaves as they scratched at her face.

Isobel was very pale and still, and there was an ugly bruise on her forehead. Elizabeth knelt beside her, taking one of her hands and squeezing it anxiously. 'Isobel? Can you hear me?'

But Isobel still lay motionless. Her eyelids did not flutter even slightly, and her hand was limp and almost lifeless. Alarm began to course through Elizabeth, and suddenly all that had happened in recent days ceased to be of any consequence. Isobel was her cousin, and something dreadful had befallen her.

'Isobel? Please answer me,' she begged, rubbing the still little hand, willing it to show some response.

Marcus and Alexander had swiftly realized that something was wrong, and now they ran around the foot of the mound. Just the briefest glance was sufficient for Marcus, who immediately turned and ordered the men to reharness the sleigh as quickly as possible.

Alexander's steps faltered for a moment as he saw Isobel, and then he came to crouch beside Elizabeth. 'What happened?' he asked, reaching out instinctively to touch Isobel's pale cheek, and then drawing his hand quickly and self-consciously back again.

'I . . . I don't know,' Elizabeth replied truthfully. 'I turned to speak to her and she'd vanished. Then I saw her lying here. She has struck her head, that much is clear, but I truly do not know how it occurred.'

Marcus came toward them, touching Alexander on the shoulder. 'Can she be moved?'

'I think so. It looks as if she has simply been knocked unconscious.' Alexander glanced at the disturbed snow and holly bushes, and his gaze fixed upon a branch that was sturdier than the others. 'I believe she struck her forehead on that,' he said, pointing.

173

At that moment Isobel stirred a little.

Alexander looked swiftly down at her. 'Isobel?'

Her eyes opened slowly, and she stared up at him in confusion, not sure where she was. Then her gaze moved to Elizabeth, who still held her hand. 'Elizabeth?' she murmured, bewildered.

'What happened, Sweeting?' Elizabeth found herself automatically reverting to the childhood name that was always used in their family.

Memory began to return, and Isobel's eyes cleared just a little. 'There were some berries, and I thought how pretty they would be on my muff. But they were out of reach, and I lost my balance. That's all I remember.'

'We think you struck your head on a branch.'

Isobel put a shaky hand to her forehead, and winced with pain as she touched the bruise.

Elizabeth squeezed her fingers comfortingly. 'We're going to take you back to the house, but first we must know if you think you've broken any bones.'

Isobel moved a little, tentatively testing each limb, then she shook her head. 'I don't think I have. I just feel very dizzy, and my head hurts.'

'It will, I fear, but you'll soon be all right again,' Elizabeth said reassuringly.

The sleigh bells jingled as the stableboy led the sleigh through the snow toward them. As it halted, Alexander scooped Isobel effortlessly into his arms, and carried her to lay her gently in the front seat where earlier she had squealed and laughed with such excitement.

Marcus assisted Elizabeth to her feet. 'Are you all right?' he asked briefly.

'Yes, thank you.'

He continued to hold her hand for a moment. 'For what it's worth, Elizabeth French, I think Alexander is a great fool, but then my opinion is possibly of no interest to you.' He conducted her toward the sleigh, and when they were all seated inside, the boy urged the team into action, leading them as swiftly as he could back toward the house.

CHAPTER 14

THE NEAREST DOCTOR resided more than two miles away, but the lanes were so blocked with snow that it was decided not to attempt to bring him to Rainworth. Marcus's cook, Mrs Harmon, who had some experience of nursing, concluded that Isobel needed only to take to her bed for a day or so after the administering of suitable medicaments, and soon all would be well again.

Elizabeth knew that this was sound advice, and so Isobel found herself being firmly compelled to do exactly as the cook instructed. Her maid, Annie, assisted her out of her clothes and into a fresh lace-trimmed nightgown, the bedroom shutters and curtains were closed, candles were lit, and the fire was built up to make the air as warm and comfortable as possible. An ointment of oil of marjoram and honey was applied to the bruise, some chamomile tea was infused to calm her and ease the headache, and some dried lavender was tucked into her pillow to assist her to sleep. Then, when the maid and the cook had withdrawn, it was Elizabeth who sat on the edge of the bed, gently brushing Isobel's hair.

Isobel toyed with the frills on the cuff of her nightgown. 'I feel so very silly. All this because I wanted a spray of holly berries.'

'These things happen, Sweeting,' murmured Elizabeth, drawing the brush slowly through the tangled chestnut curls.

Isobel smiled at her for a moment. 'It's strange to hear that pet name after all this time. I'd almost forgotten it.'

'So had I.'

'We did like each other occasionally when we were children, didn't we?'

'Occasionally.'

Isobel drew a long breath. 'I was a horrid brat, wasn't I?'

'Mostly.'

Isobel lowered her eyes, suddenly pricked with conscience. She had behaved very badly, and certainly did not deserve Elizabeth's kindness now.

Elizabeth put the hairbrush down on the table by the bed, and then stood. 'Try to sleep now. Mrs Harmon says that the chamomile tea will soon begin to take effect. How does your head feel now that the ointment has been applied?'

'It still hurts a great deal. Oh, I'm going to look dreadful, aren't I?

'Of course not.' Elizabeth held the bedclothes while Isobel snuggled down, then she tucked her in. 'I'll stay with you, so that if you need anything . . .'

Isobel took her hand suddenly. 'Thank you for being so kind to me.'

'You're my cousin,' Elizabeth replied, smiling a little.

Guilty tears stung Isobel's eyes.

Elizabeth became concerned. 'Is something wrong?' she asked quickly.

'No. I . . . I just wish my head did not hurt so much,' Isobel replied, turning her face away because she felt so full of self-reproach.

'I won't leave you,' Elizabeth promised, pausing for a moment, and then going to sit in the chair by the fire. It was a high-backed armchair covered with pink-and-white chintz, and she leaned her head back against it, closing her eyes for a moment.

The room fell silent, except for the crackling of the fire. It was a large bedroom, very Tudor in style, and was quite obviously half of a much larger chamber that had been divided by handsome wooden paneling. Isobel's bed was huge and heavy, with ornately draped green brocade curtains and heavily carved posts. The bedhead was very grand indeed, and carved and painted with the Sheridan family's coat-of-arms and lion badge. Firelight flickered warmly over the room, and outside the temperature plummeted as the afternoon drew to a close and darkness began to steal over the countryside.

The fire made Elizabeth feel drowsy, and she closed her eyes again. How strange it was that in spite of Isobel's disgraceful conduct, especially today, it was family feeling that had immediately leaped to the fore when the accident had happened. Would it still have been like that if she, Elizabeth, had really loved Alexander?

She drifted into sleep, and in her dreams she was at the Devonshire House ball again. *L'Échange* was playing, only she wasn't dancing. She stood at the side of the floor, watching everyone else. Isobel was dancing with Marcus, and Alexander was dancing with a lady whose face she could not see. The cotillion proceeded through its figures, drawing closer and closer to its conclusion. The final steps were imminent now, and still she could not make out the face of the second lady. The orchestra struck the last chords, and the dancers exchanged partners. Isobel whirled into Alexander's arms, and he kissed her passionately on the lips, crushing her so close it was as if he would hold her forever. The other lady twisted into Marcus's embrace, and he kissed her. His fingers curled luxuriously in her honey-colored hair, and as she drew away at last, her eyes dark with desire and her cheeks flushed with feeling, Elizabeth saw her face. It was Constance Bannerman.

Marcus and Alexander were in the grand chamber. It was now quite dark outside, and the cold air drew the fire so that it glowed and sparks fled up the chimney into the night. Alexander was in the chair usually occupied by Isobel, and he gratefully accepted the large glass of cognac Marcus poured for him.

Marcus watched him as he swirled the rich amber liquid. 'I fear that your stay here at Rainworth has been plagued by misfortune,' he said after a moment. 'First there was the snow, and now this.'

Alexander nodded. 'And my dealings with Elizabeth have not been all they should,' he murmured.

'In what way?' Marcus studied him carefully.

'Things have not gone well between us recently.'

'I am sure that all will be resolved.'

'Would that I could feel as certain, but I fear that there is a positive gulf between us at the moment.' Alexander smiled a little wryly. 'Sometimes it almost feels as if she is as distant from me as your Miss Bannerman is from you, except that Elizabeth and I are in the same house, but you are on the other side of the world from Miss Bannerman.'

'Do you love her?' Marcus asked bluntly.

'Yes, of course I do. What on earth prompts you to question it?'

Marcus pursed his lips for a moment. 'Forgive me if I trespass by what I am about to say, but I feel I must say it. I wonder about your feelings for Mrs French when it is clear to me that you are rather too drawn toward Lady Isobel.'

'Lady Isobel is without reproach,' Alexander declared defensively, draining his glass and getting to his feet.

Marcus did not comment upon this patently untrue statement, for Isobel was most definitely not beyond reproach, but Alexander's reaction was that of a man whose conscience was not entirely clear, and he had not denied being attracted to Isobel.

Alexander went to pour himself another glass of cognac. 'What of you and Miss Bannerman? When do you mean to return to American to marry her?'

Marcus did not reply.

Alexander looked quickly at him. 'There are problems?'

'There are always problems,' murmured Marcus, turning to lean a hand on the stone fireplace and gaze into the heart of the fire. The flames flickered over his face, and burnished his blond hair to copper.

'But you do love her?'

'I loved her from the moment I saw her.'

Alexander was curious. 'Would it help to talk about it?'

Marcus smiled. 'Thank you for the offer, my friend, but no, it would not help at all,' he replied dryly. Then he straightened. 'I think I will go to see how Lady Isobel is.' Without waiting for Alexander to comment, he turned on his heel and walked from the room.

Elizabeth awoke when she heard his quiet knock at the door. She sat up with a start, her glance moving swiftly toward the bed, but she saw immediately that Isobel was fast asleep. Getting up, she shook out the folds of her shell-pink gown, then she went quickly to the door to admit him.

'Please come in,' she said, hoping that she did not appear quite as disheveled as she felt. She had managed to put some pins back in her hair when they had returned to the house with Isobel, but there had not been any fresh combing, and so she knew she was not as well groomed as she would have wished.

He smiled a little as he saw the self-conscious way she touched her unruly curls. 'You look very well, Mrs French, please believe me,' he murmured, entering the room and looking toward the bed. 'How is Lady Isobel?'

'Sleeping, as you can see. I think that Mrs Harmon's chamomile tea was the very thing that was needed.'

'No doubt she will still have a headache when she awakens, but I'm sure she will have recovered somewhat.' He looked at Elizabeth. 'Should you not think of retiring yourself? Lady Isobel's maid could sit with her.'

'I promised Isobel I would stay.'

'She doesn't deserve it,' he replied frankly.

She colored a little. 'She is still my cousin, sir.'

'And blood is thicker than water?' he asked.

'Yes, I suppose so.'

'Is there anything you require?'

'I'm quite all right, thank you.'

He nodded. 'Than I will leave you, but please do not

hesitate to ask for whatever you wish. Good night, Mrs French.'

'Good night, sir.'

He took her hand, and raised it to his lips, but as he did so he hesitated, turning it palm uppermost.

She snatched her hand away. 'No! Please, don't!' she whispered.

'It is hardly meant as an insult,' he said.

'But it is taken as an insult, sir, an insult to me and to Miss Bannerman,' she replied angrily, for there was now no mistaking his purpose. Seduction was on his mind, nothing more and nothing less.

His blue eyes became a little cool in the candlelight. 'You know nothing about Miss Bannerman, nothing at all.'

'I do not need to, sir. Please leave now.'

'As you wish.' With a stiff bow, he turned and left.

She closed the door behind him, and then leaned back against it, fighting the tears away. She loathed herself suddenly, for she had wanted him to kiss her palm, she had wanted him to then sweep her into his arms and kiss her on the lips. She had wanted her dream to come true, and to surrender completely to him, but such abandon would be all that was wrong. No matter how precarious her betrothal to Alexander had become, it still had not been called off, and Marcus had now shown himself to be as false-hearted a womanizer as James French.

Isobel stirred in the bed, and Elizabeth put Marcus from her mind as she went quickly to her. 'Isobel?'

'Have I slept long?'

'Only a few hours. How do you feel?'

'My head isn't aching quite so much.'

'Can I get you anything?'

Isobel shook her head a little. 'No, I'll go back to sleep if I can.' She took Elizabeth's hand. 'You don't have to sit with me anymore, I'll be all right now.'

'Are you quite sure?'

'Yes. Elizabeth, you'll never know how grateful I am for the way you've taken care of me. I . . . I think you've been quite wonderful.'

'Nonsense, I've only done what I'm sure you would have done in my place.'

'I'd like to think I would, but I don't think I'm as nice a person as you,' Isobel replied.

'You make me sound like an angel, which I assure you I am not,' Elizabeth said a little wryly. 'Are you sure you'll be all right now?'

'Quite sure. Good night, Elizabeth.'

'Good night.' Elizabeth bent to kiss her on the cheek, and as she did so Isobel suddenly put her arms around her and hugged her.

When Elizabeth had gone, Isobel lay remorsefully in the bed. Her conscience had become a torment, and she could hardly believe she had behaved as she had. But it wasn't too late to put everything right. . . .

Before going to her own room, Elizabeth decided to walk a little in the gallery. She had brought a candle with her from Isobel's room, and shielded its flame with her hand as she went. As she reached the gallery, she saw immediately that someone was in the library, for the door was open and light flooded out. Her little shoes had soft soles and thus made no sound as she walked, so that she reached the library door without the occupant realizing she was there.

Looking inside, she saw that Marcus was seated at the writing desk. His back was toward her, and he did not sense her presence. He was writing a letter, but evidently it was proving difficult, for suddenly he tossed his pen aside and crumpled the sheet of paper, tossing it almost angrily across the room, where it rolled against the curtain that hung against another door. Then he picked up the miniature of his bride-to-be, and sat back in his chair studying it.

From where Elizabeth stood, she could see how his thumb moved gently over the little painted face, and then he seemed to find inspiration from somewhere, for he replaced the miniature on the desk, took another sheet of paper, and began to write again. This time the words flowed from his pen.

Elizabeth drew back, and retraced her steps along the gallery. If she had ever needed proof that Constance Bannerman was part of his life, she had seen it in the tender way he had caressed the miniature. But even though it was plain that he loved Constance, he had still embarked upon seduction here at Rainworth. He was worthless, as worthless as James had proved to be.

CHAPTER 15

IT WAS STILL fine, clear, and cold the next morning. The overnight temperature had been arctic, and when the sun rose its rays had barely touched the chill that lay over the frozen landscape. The snow still lay as deep and impassable as before, and the whole of England was caught in its icy trap.

Elizabeth rose early, and was relieved to hear from Violet that Isobel was very much better. She still had a headache, but that was only to be expected, and she intended to get up a little later.

Putting on a warm gown of peach-colored fustian, Elizabeth then sat at the dressing table for Violet to comb and pin her hair. The maid's fingers were deft, easily twisting the heavy dark-blond curls up into a dainty knot, and then combing out a number of thin ringlets. When the final pin was in place, Elizabeth went to the window seat, intending to try to read for a while before going down to the breakfast room, but as she glanced out of the window at the terrace, she suddenly felt the urge to go out into the fresh air. It was an idle impulse, but one she did not resist, and so a minute or so later she stepped outside, holding her aquamarine cloak closely around her as the chill morning air breathed over Rainworth.

She shivered as she walked across the terrace to the stone balustrade. The snow had mostly been cleared away now, and a layer of ice crunched beneath her overshoes. She paused by one of the stone Grecian urns at the top of the steps that led down into the topiary garden. Not all of the snow had been cleared from the foot of the steps, and she could see the marks where Alexander and Isobel had thrown snowballs the day before.

As she gazed down, she suddenly heard steps on the ice behind her, and she whirled about to see Marcus walking toward her. She stiffened defensively, meaning to be very much on her guard with him, and to tell him what she thought of him if he transgressed by so much as a single word. But even now, when she knew him to be a philanderer, she was conscious of her pulse quickening merely at the sight of him.

Few men could have appeared more to advantage in the close-fitting clothes that were all the mode now, for he had the height and shape to carry them off superbly. In spite of the cold he had not donned a greatcoat, and the coat he wore was made of a deep-blue wool with a high stand-fall collar made of black velvet. His long legs were encased in cream corduroy breeches, his top boots boasted an immaculate shine, and his golden brocade waistcoat seemed to reflect the color of his hair. The front of his shirt was adorned with two precise rows of small frills, and his blue silk neckcloth was finished with a sapphire pin.

Afraid that he might read her thoughts in her eyes, she turned back to look at the garden. 'Good morning, Your Grace,' she said in a civil but far from inviting tone.

'Good morning.'

She surveyed the garden, and then the park beyond. 'Do you really mean to sell Rainworth?' she inquired, determined to keep all conversation on a safe subject.

'It was a notion that passed my mind not so long ago, but now I do not think I will.'

She had to look at him. 'Does that mean you will bring your bride here after all?'

'My bride?'

'Miss Bannerman.'

'Ah, yes. Miss Bannerman,' he murmured, brushing some snow from the stone urn.

'She is very beautiful.'

'From which observation I must conclude that you have seen her portrait in the library.' His tone was dry.

'Yes.'

'Such miniatures are interesting mementos, are they not?'

'Mementos?'

He nodded. 'Of times past.'

She stared at him. 'What are you saying?'

'That just as I once entertained a notion of selling Rainworth, so I also entertained a notion of making Constance my bride. Both notions have been consigned to perdition.'

Confused, she searched his face. 'But you told us—'

'If you recall with any accuracy, what I said was that there was an element of truth in the below-stairs gossip you and Lady Isobel had heard,' he interrupted.

She lowered her eyes, for that was indeed what he had said. 'Are you telling me that we formed the wrong conclusion?'

'Yes. Constance and I are no longer to be married, and with

187

the benefit of hindsight I can see that if we had it would have been a considerable mismatch, just as I can tell that if you and Alexander marry, it will be a similar disaster.'

She drew sharply back. 'Sir, I do not wish to discuss such things with you.'

'How very tiresome, for I intend to see that such things are just what you do discuss with me,' he replied tersely, catching her arm as she made to walk past him.

'Unhand me,' she breathed angrily, but even as she tried to remain on her dignity, she was aware of his closeness. Was there no refuge from his spell?

'You're going to hear me out, Elizabeth, because I can no longer keep silent. I am a far from disinterested party in all this, indeed the only reason you and the others are here at all is because I want you. Is that sufficiently direct and to the point?' His blue eyes were arresting in the cold sunlight, and he still held her arm so firmly that she could not pull away.

But she didn't struggle, for his words rendered her motion-less. 'What did you say?' she whispered.

'I said that I want you, Elizabeth, and I believe I have done so since the night I rescued you from the footpads.' He released her then. 'When I saw you alighting from Alexander's carriage in Grantham, I could not believe my eyes. After having given up all hope of ever finding out who you were, I found myself looking at you getting out of my old friend's carriage. Then I saw him with Lady Isobel, and by their manner together, I concluded that she was the Mrs French I had heard he was to marry. When I spoke to him, and he said that he and Mrs French were chaperoning Lady Isobel Crawford to Southwell Park, I naturally believed that you were Lady Isobel, a free agent to whom I could pay court if such approaches were welcome. That was why I pressed Alexander to accept my invitation, and why you were taken to be your cousin when you arrived here. When I learned the truth, I tried to put you from my thoughts, but it was not easy, especially when I very swiftly perceived how things lay between Alexander and Lady Isobel, and when I also perceived that your feelings for Alexander were not what they should be if you were to marry him. And so I am now pressing my own suit, Elizabeth, for I know that I am the man for you, if you will have me.'

She stared at him, a million breathless emotions tumbling through her. 'You . . . you seem very sure of me, sir,' she said in a trembling voice.

'I am.'

'How can you be? I have never said anything to make you—'

'True, you have never said anything, but are words always necessary?' He smiled a little, the blue of his eyes seeming to deepen. 'I am sure of you, Elizabeth,' he said softly, 'and I will prove it.'

He drew her toward him, pulling her into an embrace that seemed to envelop her very soul. His lips were urgent upon hers, and she met his kiss with all the passion that had been aroused the first moment she had glimpsed him in Hanover Square. Desire warmed her skin, and made the blood rush wildly through her veins. She clung to him, her lips parting beneath his, her heart pounding next to his. He crushed her close, as if he would devour her, and then he drew slowly back, cupping her flushed face in his hands as he looked into her eyes.

'I am sure of you, Elizabeth,' he whispered, his thumbs

189

caressing her skin. 'You're mine, not Alexander's, and I do not mean to let you escape, not until you have consented to be my bride.'

Her breath caught. 'Your bride?'

'Nothing less will do. I want you, body and soul I want you.' He bent his head to kiss her tenderly on the lips again. 'Say yes, Elizabeth,' he murmured. 'Just say yes, for I know that you love me as much as I love you.'

Ecstasy swept her along. Everything she had yearned for, but which she had thought must be denied, was now hers. This man was hers . . . 'Yes,' she whispered. 'Yes, I will marry you.'

He gathered her into his arms again, and she raised her lips to meet his.

As Elizabeth acknowledged her feelings for Marcus, Isobel was seated in the chair by the fire in her room. Her dark-chestnut hair was brushed loose about the shoulders of her daffodil-yellow wrap, and there was a blanket over her knees. She was waiting for Alexander, to whom she had sent an urgent message. Her eyes were sad, and the bruise on her forehead looked livid against her pale, wan little face.

There was a tap at the door, and Isobel's maid hurried to answer it. It was Alexander, and as he entered, the maid went discreetly out, closing the door and leaving them alone together.

He hesitated for a moment, waiting until he heard the maid's footsteps die away along the passage, and then he went to Isobel, bending to kiss her on the cheek, but she averted her head so that his lips brushed her hair.

He straightened, his eyes concerned. 'Is something wrong?'

'Yes.'

'What is it?' He bent toward her, taking her cold hands in his.

She twisted them free again. 'Please, don't, for I cannot bear it,' she whispered, her voice quivering with unhappiness.

'Have I said something wrong? Have I done something to offend you?'

'You? Oh, no, not you!' she replied quickly, meeting his anxious eyes. 'Please do not think that it is your fault, for I know that if I had not behaved as badly as I did, none of this would have happened. Oh, Alexander, I feel so ashamed, for I have conducted myself very improperly.'

'Please don't say that, for it isn't true.'

'Isn't it? Alexander, I have been quite shameless. I set my cap at you and I pursued you in a way that was unbecoming to say the least. I decided that I had to have you for myself, and I set about achieving just that. I even went so far as to deliberately turn your differences with Elizabeth to my own advantage. And then yesterday, oh, yesterday I was almost on the verge of embracing you right in front of her, just embracing you, and making it plain to the world that I was taking you from her.' Tears wended their way down her cheeks. 'I feel wretched, Alexander, and I wish with all my heart that I had not done any of the things I did.'

'It takes two, you know,' he said softly, putting his hand to her cheek.

'You would never have glanced at me if I had not forced myself upon you. You were as in love with Elizabeth as it was possible to be, but things were just a little wrong between you, and I made the most of the situation. I made myself fascinating, and I used every trick and wile I could think of in

191

order to win you.'

'And you have won me. We both know it to be true, and to pretend otherwise is pointless.'

'No, it is not pointless, Alexander, for we *must* pretend otherwise. I have to right the wrong I have done to Elizabeth, for I cannot bear to know how badly I have treated her. She has been so kind to me, indeed no one could have been more kind, and now I cannot live with my conscience. We must stop everything, Alexander.'

'You cannot mean this,' he cried, straightening and running his hand through his dark hair.

'I do mean it. You and Elizabeth are to be betrothed soon, and that betrothal must go ahead as planned. You must forget me, just as I must forget you.'

'Isobel, I wish you would reconsider, for I love you.'

'You belong to Elizabeth, and I will not be the instrument of breaking her heart. I would despise myself forever more if I persisted with this now. Go back to her, Alexander. Please, I beg of you.'

He fought away tears.

She sat forward, looking urgently at him. 'You do still love her, in spite of what you feel for me.

'Yes, I love her, and I always will, but it isn't the love I feel for you.'

Her lips trembled. 'I ... I will not change my mind, Alexander. I am ending things between us, and nothing on earth will alter it. Promise me that you will be all that you should be to Elizabeth.'

He took a long breath to steady himself. 'If that is what you truly wish?'

'It has to be.'

'Very well.' Unable to bear it a moment longer, he turned and hurried from the room.

The moment he had gone, Isobel hid her face in her hands, her shoulders shaking as she wept. It had been the hardest thing she had ever done in her life, and the greatest sacrifice, but her honor demanded nothing less. Her honor? Oh, better to find it late than never to find it at all.

She lowered her hands, striving to control the sobs that still rose so miserably in her throat. Her glance fell upon the volume of *Childe Harold's Pilgrimage*, which her maid had that very day unpacked and placed on the little table by the fireside chair. Suddenly she loathed the book, loathed it so much that she could not bear to see it. If it had not been for her infatuation with Lord Byron's odious hero, none of this would have happened. Snatching the volume up, she flung it on to the fire, watching as the flames licked eagerly around the elegant leather binding.

Shortly afterward, Elizabeth awaited Alexander in the library. She had sent Violet to find him, to tell him she wished to speak to him on a matter of some urgency and importance, and the library seemed a suitable place for a meeting that she knew was going to be awkward. Marcus had wanted to be with her, but she had insisted upon being alone when she told Alexander that she no longer intended to proceed with their match. She did not think that Alexander was going to be displeased with what she said, for she was sure in her heart that he now loved Isobel, but she knew that he was going to be surprised to learn of her love for Marcus.

She was nervous as she waited, and she could not sit down, but paced a little, pausing every now and then to look at the shelves of handsome book spines. Oh, please hurry, Alexander, she thought, for the suspense was quite dreadful. She wished it all to be over and done with, and she hoped with all her heart that the conclusion would be what they all four really wished. A fitting ending to their own private cotillion here in the Nottinghamshire countryside.

As she paced, her foot brushed against something on the floor. She glanced down and saw that it was the letter Marcus had been writing the night before. She stared down at it, for although it was crumpled into a ball, she could still make out some of the words. *My very dearest Constance....*

Slowly she bent to pick it up. No, please don't let this be.... She didn't want to read the letter, but knew that she must. Her hands shook as she smoothed the paper.

> *My very dearest Constance,*
> *Forgive me for having delayed so long in writing to you, but as you may imagine, I have had a great deal on my mind since arriving here. I have been sorely missing our private moments in the summerhouse, and I long for your laughing eyes and happy society. I cannot write more without coming directly to the heart of the matter, by which I mean our marriage plans ...*

It was here that Marcus had discarded the letter, and thrown it away for its incriminating words to expose him now. She had been taken for a fool, oh, what a fool! He had lied to her about Constance, and his only possible reason was that he still had mere seduction in mind for gullible Elizabeth French.

Her hands were shaking so much that she could barely screw the hated letter into a ball again. He wasn't going to succeed in his vile intentions, for she was a fool no more.

Footsteps approached the door, and she whirled about in dismay, praying that it was not Marcus, for she wasn't ready to face him yet. Not yet. But then she recognized Alexander's tread.

CHAPTER 16

THE LETTER SLIPPED from her fingers, and her hands were still trembling so much that she had to clasp them before her. The things she had planned to say to him suddenly fled from her head, and for a moment she was all confusion and near panic, but then she took a grip on herself. The fact that her foolishness had brought her close to disaster did not make any real difference to what she must say to Alexander. Any thought of a contract between them would be a dreadful mistake, and she had to release him without any further delay.

He entered, pausing in the doorway for a moment. She thought he looked a little drawn, and even at a moment such as this she was conscious of the wry reflection that his pallor and looks did indeed bring Childe Harold to mind.

He closed the door quietly. 'You wished to see me, Elizabeth?'

'Yes, for I think it is time we spoke frankly to each other.'

The ghost of a smile touched his lips. 'Surely it was frank speaking that brought us to this pitch.'

'We have both been at fault, I think.'

He nodded, coming toward her and taking her hand, enclosing it in both his. 'I am so sorry for some of the things I've said to you. I swear that I will not behave so badly in future. It is most definitely time to call a halt.'

'Yes, it is.'

'There must not be any further misunderstandings.'

'I agree.' She smiled.

'Our future together is far too important and precious to throw it away because of foolish disagreements,' he went on.

She stared at him. Their future together? She had thought he was speaking of ending their match, but instead it seemed he wished it to continue!

He looked at her in concern. 'Is something wrong?'

'I . . . Alexander, I did not think, I mean, I thought . . .' She couldn't find the words, for she had been so sure that he would want to withdraw.

'What did you think?'

She gave a half-laugh. 'I thought you wished to end our match.'

'End it? No, of course not. Oh, I realize that some of the things I've said may have pointed to such a course, but I did not mean it. Everything has seemed so uncertain and difficult recently, and I am afraid that I have not been dealing with it as well as I should. For that you must forgive me.'

She searched his face. 'Alexander, when you came in I said that I thought it was time for a little frank speaking. May I therefore be frank with you?'

He nodded. 'Of course.'

'Then I will tell you that I really expected you to wish to

withdraw because you now feel more for Isobel than you feel for me.'

He met her gaze squarely. 'There is nothing between Isobel and me, Elizabeth. We are friends, good friends, but that is all there is to it. Please believe me.'

'But, I was so sure.' She turned away, completely confounded by his words. 'I would have sworn on oath that Isobel was in love with you, and although I was never quite so sure about your feelings for her, I had come to believe that you were indeed becoming more and more drawn to her. Are you telling me that I have been wrong in every way?'

He hesitated. 'I – er – I think you may have been right about Isobel, at least for a while. I believe she was a little impressed with my so-called resemblance to Byron's wretched creation, but when she realized that I did not in any way match up to Childe Harold, she soon ceased to be impressed. It was a fleeting fancy, no more than that, and it never meant anything. She would be very embarrassed and ashamed if she thought you believed her guilty of any misdemeanor.'

Elizabeth pressed her hands to her cheeks, trying to sort her scattered thoughts. 'And this is the truth?'

His gaze was still steady. 'Yes, it is the truth. I do not wish to end our match, Elizabeth, and I hope that we can put all this behind us.' He smiled, putting his hand to her cheek. 'Let us take each day at a time, and then we will be able to slowly mend the damage. What we have is too good to discard without a struggle. Maybe we are not the world's greatest love match, but we do love each other, and if it is not a love of towering passion and breathless ecstasy, it is still more than sufficient for us to be very happy together. I want you to be my wife, Elizabeth. Please say that you wish the same.'

Put all this behind them? Oh, if only that were possible.

'We should go on, Elizabeth, for whatever has gone wrong recently, it is not insurmountable. If there was not sufficient feeling between us, we would not be able to speak to each other like this, would we?'

A lump rose in her throat, and she gave him a rather shaky smile. 'Oh, Alexander, you will always mean a great deal to me.'

'And you to me. So, is it agreed? We proceed as before?'

She hardly knew that she had nodded her consent, she only knew that he had pulled her into his embrace. His lips were gentle against her forehead, and she closed her eyes, drawing immeasurable comfort from his tenderness. How she wished she had never set eyes on Marcus Sheridan, false-hearted Duke of Arlingham, how she wished he had never stirred old longings for James, how she wished ... Oh, there were so many regrets now. She and Alexander could be happy together, they would be happy together.

But as she raised her lips to meet his kiss, it was still Marcus that her perfidious heart longed for, and as Alexander bent his head toward her, it was Isobel he really held.

Elizabeth had arranged to meet Marcus in the breakfast room once she had spoken to Alexander, and now she went down the staircase to keep the assignation. A dark anger burned through her that he had behaved so dishonorably, and she intended to disillusion him if he should be so smug as to imagine he would still succeed with her. She despised him for his shallow immorality, and she despised herself for permitting him the liberties he had taken.

At the bottom of the staircase she halted for a moment, screwing herself up to the necessary pitch for what was bound to be a very unpleasant interview. Then, taking a deep breath, she walked toward the door of the breakfast room.

He was standing by the window, as he had been on her first morning there, and he turned with a quick smile as she entered. Beyond the window the snow was now tinged with blue as the afternoon sun began to sink toward the west, and long shadows reached across the ground, as if intent upon stretching as far as they could before darkness swallowed them.

Marcus's smile faded as he saw the anger on her face. 'What is it?' he asked, coming quickly toward her, but as he went to take her hands, she drew sharply back.

'Don't touch me,' she breathed. 'Don't ever touch me again! I loathe you, my lord duke, for you are everything that is mean and despicable.'

His eyes became cool, but there was no mistaking the puzzlement in them. 'I trust you mean to explain this *volte face?*'

'You have been found out, sirrah. Your lies are now manifest, and I have merely kept this assignation in order to tell you what I think of you.'

'I have not lied to you, Elizabeth.'

'Oh, yes you have, for you have lied about Miss Bannerman, who far from being a figure from the past, is very much a figure in your future! No doubt you hoped that I would prove to be a simple conquest, perhaps even that I might be persuaded to grace your bed while we are incarcerated here, but I am afraid that your mean designs have come to naught, for I am no longer even remotely likely to surrender to you.'

'If you recall, Elizabeth, far from treating you with dishonor, I have actually asked you to be my wife, and as to having lied to you about Constance, I can only say again that she and I are most definitely not intending to spend our future together.'

'Don't attempt to gull me any more, sirrah, for each further deceit makes you more contemptible. I merely wish to tell you that I am now completely immune to your advances, and that Alexander and I have resolved our differences. We still mean to proceed with our match, sirrah, for just as you were wrong to see me as easy prey, so you were equally wrong about Isobel and him.'

His blue eyes were now ice-cold. 'You are very free with your insults, madam.'

'With every justification!'

'Indeed? Well, let me tell you yet again that I do not have any contract or understanding with Constance, and that—'

'I have read your letter to her,' she interrupted.

'Letter?'

'The one you found so difficult to write, and discarded before writing another.'

A light passed through his gaze. 'Ah, yes, that letter. And that is your reason for these charges against me?'

'It is more than sufficient reason,' she replied coldly.

'You would certainly appear to think so,' he murmured.

'Are you going to deny writing it?'

'No.'

She raised her chin, hating him for what he had done. 'I

bitterly regret allowing you to come so close to me, sirrah, for now I feel—'

'You go too far, Elizabeth!' he snapped. 'Believe what you wish, if that is your pleasure, but I have endured sufficient insult. So you are immune to my advances, are you? Well, we will see about that!'

Before she knew what was happening, he had seized her wrist, jerking her roughly into his arms. He forced his lips upon hers, his fingers hard upon the nape of her neck as he held her head. She could not move, for he was far too strong, and his kiss was relentless, burning upon her lips as if he meant to sear her with his fury.

His arm moved like iron around her waist, pressing her body against his so that his anger seemed to invade her. There was no gentleness in him, but there was skill. Oh, there was skill. For all their force, his lips teased hers, and for all its strength, his embrace stirred her unwilling senses. She hated him, she hated him with all her heart, but she wanted him as well! She tried to push him away, to deny the feelings he even now seemed able to arouse in her, but she could not. In spite of everything she now knew, she found herself responding to him. Tears stung her eyes, but her lips softened beneath his, parting a little as she gave way to the rich desire that had begun to overtake her whole being.

With a cold laugh he thrust her away. 'So that is your notion of being immune to me, is it? Forgive me if I find that somewhat amusing, madam!'

Betrayed alike by his deceit and by her own weakness, she struck out, dealing him a stinging blow to the cheek. His head jerked aside, and she would have struck him again, but he caught her arm.

'Enough, Elizabeth,' he breathed, his blue eyes dark and bright at the same time.

'I hate you,' she whispered.

'I think not, but believe it if it is your notion of amusement. You will never be over me, and you will never forget me, I promise you.'

Her eyes shone with helpless tears. 'Maybe I will not forget you, sir, but nor will I forgive you.'

'I have not done anything for which I require to be forgiven, madam. I don't know how Alexander has pulled the wool over your eyes about Isobel, but that is what he has done, for *she* is the one he really wants, and I warn you that she more than returns his feelings. As to my so-called understanding with Constance, well its nonexistence is very simple to prove, but since you are so easily disposed to believe me to be lying, I do not think I will bother to clear my name. Go to Alexander if you wish, but if it is me you want, then you will have to come to me.'

'I would as soon go to the devil!' she cried.

'Then go!' He released her.

Gathering her skirts, she ran from the room. Tears almost blinded her, and sobs caught in her throat as she hurried up the staircase and along the gallery.

When she reached the privacy of her room she flung herself on the bed, hiding her face in the pillows as she wept brokenheartedly.

In the breakfast room, Marcus's face was very pale and taut, and a nerve flickered at his temple as he went to the window and stared out. His heart felt as cold as the snow, and he could still hear her voice whispering in the room. *I hate you, I hate you, I hate you. . . .*

For a long moment he continued to gaze out, but at last he lowered his eyes. 'Oh, Elizabeth,' he murmured. 'It cannot be left like this, but has to be resolved once and for all if this damned cotillion of ours is to be satisfactorily concluded.'

Turning on his heel, he strode purposefully from the room.

Isobel was sitting by the fire in her room. She wasn't crying now, but her eyes were tearstained. She felt hollow, for even though she was sure she had at last done the proper thing, she could not escape from the love she had for the man she had sent back to her cousin.

There was a knock at the door, and her maid went to answer it. She returned in a moment. 'It's the duke, Lady Isobel.'

Isobel's heart sank, for she did not want to receive visitors at the moment, but there was nothing for it but to admit him. 'Please show him in,' she replied.

He came in, his quick glance taking in the marks of her tears. 'You and I should speak, Lady Isobel,' he said quietly.

She hesitated, and then dismissed the maid. 'That is all for the moment, Annie,' she said.

'My lady.' Annie curtsied and discreetly withdrew, closing the door softly behind her.

Isobel looked at Marcus again. 'What is it you wish to say to me, sir?'

'I have a rather delicate proposition to put to you, Lady Isobel, and all I ask is that you hear me out before replying.'

'A delicate proposition?'

'Very delicate, and very important,' he replied, with a glimmer of a smile. 'You may be shocked and offended, or, on the other hand, you may realize that what I am about to suggest would be very much to your own personal advantage. Will you hear me out?'

She searched his face for a long moment, and then slowly nodded. 'Yes, my lord duke, I will hear you out.'

CHAPTER 17

MARCUS LEANED ON his billiard cue, watching as Alexander
bent to make a shot. They were whiling away a little time
before dinner, and both wore evening clothes. It was now
quite dark outside.

The billiard room lay on the western side of the house,
beyond the grand chamber, and its windows overlooked the
part of the park where the *montagne Russe* stood among the
pine trees. It was a small room, and a log fire roared in the
hearth of the stone fireplace, warming the still air so much
that both men had removed their coats and played in their
shirts and white satin waistcoats. A ceiling lamp was
suspended low over the green felt surface of the table, and it
was a concentrated light that left most of the room in shadow,
except for the dancing light from the fire.

Alexander's mind wasn't on the game, for he muffed the
shot even after he had taken a great deal of time about it. The
ivory cue ball rolled aimlessly across the green felt, coming to
rest fruitlessly against the cushion that surrounded the playing surface. With an impatient snort, he put his cue down in

a final manner. 'I'll have to cry off, Marcus, for I simply cannot concentrate.'

'So I've noticed, for you've given me nearly every chance I can think of,' replied Marcus, taking both their cues and replacing them on the rack on the wall. 'Cognac?' he asked.

'Yes. Thank you.' Alexander went to the fireplace, leaning a hand on the mantelpiece and then pressing one of the logs down with his boot.

Marcus poured two generous glasses from a crystal decanter on a nearby table, and then gave one to his friend. 'What's bothering you, Alexander? You seem – er – distracted.'

'Oh, it's nothing of any real consequence.'

'That isn't how it appears to me, indeed I would say that it is something of considerable consequence. Would it help to talk about it?'

'It would, but I cannot. It's better if I say nothing at all, for the problem is not mine alone to bear.'

'It concerns Elizabeth as well?'

Alexander nodded, not noticing the use of her first name only.

'When we spoke in the grand chamber yesterday evening, you mentioned that there was a gulf between you. Am I to take it that that gulf is still there?'

'Yes. No. Oh, I don't know.' Alexander drained his glass in one gulp. 'I wish it was simple, but it isn't, and I'm desperately afraid of doing the wrong thing.'

'My friend, let me give you a word of sound advice. Follow the dictates of your heart, and you will not go far wrong.'

Alexander looked at him. 'Is it advice you follow yourself?'

'Yes, never more so than now.'

Alexander could not say anything more, for there was a tap at the door, and Isobel's maid came shyly in. She gave him a neat curtsy. 'Begging your pardon, Sir Alexander, but Lady Isobel wishes to see you.'

'See me?'

'Yes, sir. She says that it is very important that she speaks to you before dinner.'

'Very well, I will go to her now.'

'She is in the great hall, sir.' Annie lowered her eyes.

He was taken aback. 'The great hall?'

'Yes, sir.'

Puzzled as to why Isobel would choose such a public place to speak to him, he turned to Marcus. 'If you will excuse me. . . ?'

'By all means.'

Replacing his glass on the table, Alexander snatched up his coat and hurried out. Annie lingered for a moment, waiting until he had gone, and then looking inquiringly at Marcus.

'Shall I go to Mrs French now, Your Grace?'

'No, give Lady Isobel at least five minutes.'

'Your Grace.' Curtsying again, the maid went out.

Marcus swirled his cognac, and then drank it. The maid had arrived exactly on cue. On cue? How singularly appropriate that phrase was. He stretched across the table and rolled the ivory cue ball toward the corner pocket. As it fell satisfactorily into its allotted place, he smiled. It was only to be hoped that everything else would be as obliging before this most important night was over.

He put his glass down on the table, and then went to pick up his black velvet coat from the chair where he had left it earlier. He put it on, and then teased the lace frills of his shirt from the tight cuffs. In five minutes or so he would know whether his plan was going to work.

Taking a deep breath, he left the billiard room, but he did not follow Alexander through the grand chamber, instead he went in a different direction, taking a small back staircase that would bring him out on the minstrels' gallery above the hall. From there he would be able to observe everything as it unfolded.

As Alexander crossed the grand chamber, he heard someone playing the piano in the hall. He emerged through the arched doorway and paused as he saw that it was Isobel. She looked breathtakingly beautiful in a pale green silk evening gown that had dainty silver spangles scattered over its high-waisted bodice. The gown's neckline was low and daring, showing off how slender and willowy she was, and her hair was swept up into a graceful and very fashionable knot at the back of her head. Diamonds flashed at her pale throat, and the bruise on her forehead had been rendered almost invisible by the judicious application of a little color from her Chinese cosmetic box.

She seemed to be unaware of his presence as she played a lilting melody that he recognized as vaguely familiar, but could not quite place. As he went slowly toward the dais, she saw him, and a soft smile curved her lovely lips. She continued to play, and at last he realized what tune it was. She was playing *L'Échange*.

She gazed at him as he came up the few steps on to the dais, and her playing proceeded without faltering as he leaned an elbow on the piano, smiling down into her eyes. The refrain of the cotillion rippled over the vastness of the candlelit hall, where the suits of armor stood like a silent but appreciative audience.

The final notes died away, and she spoke in the ensuing silence. 'I had to speak to you,' she said softly.

'I thought it had all been said,' he replied, loving her so much that he could barely restrain himself from sweeping her up into his arms.

'I know what I said, and I know that it is very wrong to love you as I do, but I cannot help myself. Alexander, I must be with you, for without you I fear I shall wither away.'

She reached out tentatively toward him, and in a moment his fingers had closed convulsively over hers.

Elizabeth was seated before the dressing table in her rooms as Violet pushed the final pin into her coiffure. The last thing she felt like was facing Marcus at the dinner table, but she knew that that was what she must do. She gazed at her reflection in the small mirror before her, and saw that although she had applied a little rouge to her cheeks, a little more was still needed if she was to appear cheerful and unperturbed.

Violet had taken great care with her hair, teasing little curls around her forehead, and twisting the longer tresses back into a loose knot from which fell one plump, curling ringlet. The gown she had chosen was made of cornflower-blue taffeta with little petal sleeves, and its low square neckline was trimmed with golden embroidery. Her only jewelry was the pair of gold earrings Marcus had regained for her.

She was just applying a little of her favorite lavender water when there was a knock at the outer door. 'See who it is, Violet,' she said.

'Madam.' Putting the comb down, the maid hurried

through to the other room.

Elizabeth heard a female voice, and thought it sounded like Isobel's maid. Getting up, she went into the bedroom. 'What is it, Violet?'

'Lady Isobel is feeling a little unwell, madam. She went down to the hall and became faint. She wishes you to go to her straightaway.'

'Yes, of course,' replied Elizabeth without hesitation.

Violet brought her her shawl, and a moment later Elizabeth had picked up a lighted candle and hurried from the room.

Violet expected Annie to go with her, but instead the other maid held back, showing no inclination at all to return to her mistress. 'Shouldn't you go to Lady Isobel?' Violet asked, puzzled.

'There's no need, because there isn't anything wrong with her,' Annie replied.

Violet's jaw dropped. 'Nothing wrong with her? But you just said—'

'I was doing as Lady Isobel bade me, and as the duke bade me as well,' the maid added.

'The duke? But what has he to do with it?'

'Everything, for it was his idea.'

'What was his idea?' demanded Violet in exasperation.

'The plan to see that my mistress wins Sir Alexander, and he, the duke, wins Mrs French,' Annie replied simply.

Violet stared at her.

Shielding the fluttering candle with her hand, Elizabeth walked swiftly along the deserted gallery. The library was in darkness, but the door was again ajar, and as she passed the light from her candle fell briefly across the desk, illuminating

211

the miniature of Constance Bannerman, which still stood in its former prominent place.

Elizabeth hastened on, for the library held bitter memories of a half-finished letter and the discovery of falsehood in the man to whom she had so foolishly and easily surrendered her heart.

At last she reached the top of the grand staircase, but there she halted abruptly, her gaze immediately drawn to the dais, where she saw Isobel and Alexander by the piano. Isobel's spangles and diamonds flashed in the glow from the hall's many candles, and even from that distance Elizabeth could see the warm flush on her cheeks as she smiled up into Alexander's eyes. Far from appearing faint and wilting, Lady Isobel Crawford looked remarkably well.

As Elizabeth watched, Alexander suddenly pulled Isobel to her feet and into his arms. He kissed her passionately on the lips, pressing her slender body against his. Isobel linked her arms around his neck as she eagerly submitted to the embrace.

Elizabeth stared down at them, and then suddenly she became aware of a shadowy movement on the minstrels' gallery above their heads. She raised her eyes, and found herself meeting Marcus's steady, deliberate gaze.

She backed away from the top of the staircase, and then tore her eyes from his as she turned to hurry back toward her room.

On the dais, Isobel drew swiftly back from Alexander, and turned to look up at the gallery overhead. 'Was it well done?' she asked.

As Marcus leaned his hands on the balustrade and looked down, Alexander leaped back as if scalded. Guilty color rushed into his face, and he looked reproachfully at Isobel.

Marcus nodded at her. 'It was well done. Now the rest is up to me.' His eyes swung to meet Alexander's. 'Continue to take my advice, my friend. Follow the dictates of your heart, just as I do.'

As Marcus left the gallery, Alexander looked accusingly at Isobel. 'What is going on? What have you done?'

'I have been entirely honest, and I have seen to it that you have been as well. Elizabeth was at the top of the staircase a moment or so ago, and she saw us together.'

Alexander closed his eyes. 'And you think that that was something well done?' he breathed.

She took his hands. 'Yes, Alexander, I do, for you and I belong together, just as Elizabeth belongs with Marcus.'

He stared at her. 'With Marcus?'

She nodded. 'It's a long story, but one which I hope with all my heart will end as we all wish.' She looked toward the top of the staircase, where now there were only shadows. 'I pray that Elizabeth will hear him out, for her happiness depends upon it.'

Alexander ran his hand perplexedly through his hair. 'I think you should explain all this to me.'

'I will, sir, for a small price,' she replied coquettishly.

'A small price?'

'Kiss me again, and then I will tell you whatever you wish to know.' She linked her arms around his neck once more, stretching up toward his lips.

He could not resist her, and once again pulled her into his arms.

Elizabeth's taffeta gown rustled as she hurried back to her room. Violet and Annie were still talking as she approached, and Annie quickly left, pausing only to bob a polite curtsy to Elizabeth as they passed, but Elizabeth did not even glance at her.

Violet stood aside for her mistress to enter. 'Is something wrong, madam?' she asked anxiously, seeing how pale Elizabeth was.

Putting the candlestick down, Elizabeth turned to face her. 'Violet, I begin to think that nothing will ever be right again.'

'Is there anything I can do, madam?' Violet closed the door and went quickly to her.

Elizabeth gave her a small smile. 'No, thank you, Violet. Oh, except see to it that all callers are kept out. I could not possibly speak to anyone tonight.'

'Very well, madam.' The maid watched sadly as Elizabeth went to sit in the chair by the fire. The careful plan that Annie had described had evidently not worked as it should, for no one could have looked more unhappy and low than her mistress did now.

The room was so quiet that they both distinctly heard male footsteps approaching along the passage outside. Elizabeth sat forward anxiously. 'Don't admit anyone, Violet.'

'I won't, madam.'

But as the maid answered the single knock, there was no chance to refuse entry, for Marcus had more than anticipated what Elizabeth's instructions would be, and so he strode past the maid and confronted Elizabeth.

'I will not waste words, madam, but since I have now proved to you that Alexander and Isobel are far from uninterested in each other, perhaps it is now time to also correct certain other erroneous notions you appear to have. It pleased you to read my private correspondence, and to judge me

214

upon its imagined content, and so now I actually *request* you to read this second letter.' He held up a folded sheet of paper that bore a broken wax seal.

She rose slowly to her feet. 'What possible purpose will be served by pursuing this matter, sir? Why can you not simply desist? I now accept beyond all shadow of doubt that Alexander and Isobel are in love with each other, and I can assure you that I have no intention at all of attempting to stand between them. They are entirely at liberty to be together, and I only wish that Alexander had been more truthful with me this morning.'

'As truthful as you were with him?'

She colored. 'Or as you were with me?' she countered.

'Oh, I have been truthful, Elizabeth, believe me, I have. Please read this letter, and if there is then anything you feel you wish to say to me, you will find me in the library.' He pressed the letter into her unwilling hand, and then turned to walk out again.

Violet closed the door again, and then looked guiltily at her mistress. 'I couldn't stop him, madam, for he just walked straight past me.'

'It wasn't your fault, Violet,' Elizabeth replied quickly. She gazed down at the letter. It was addressed to Marcus's American residence, and had been sent to him by Constance Bannerman. She hesitated. Part of her wanted desperately to read the contents, but part of her was afraid that its words would not banish all trace of doubt. She felt bruised by all that had happened, and now she did not know if she could place her trust in anyone.

Violet came closer. 'You must read it, madam,' she ventured suddenly.

215

Elizabeth looked at her in surprise. 'Why do you say that?'

'Because the duke loves you, madam, and because I think you love him.' The maid lowered her eyes a little nervously for she knew that she had overstepped the invisible line that separated what was permissible from what was not.

Elizabeth searched her face. 'What makes you think the duke loves me?'

'He told Lady Isobel that he did, Lady Isobel told Annie, and Annie told me.'

If the whole matter had not been so serious, Elizabeth would have smiled at such a response. Was there anyone here at Rainworth who did *not* know the story of tangled love in which all four persons above-stairs had been involved over the past few days?

'Please read it, madam,' the maid pressed.

Elizabeth unfolded the sheet of paper, and began to read.

My dear Marcus,

I know that you will find it hard to forgive me for betraying your love as I have, and I freely admit that everything has been my fault, but please believe me when I say that I did not ever wish to hurt you. I should not have seen Henry Devenish when I had already pledged to marry you, but I could not help myself. I loved him before I met you, but he did not then return my affection. When I met him again, and he saw me with new eyes, I could not help myself. I know that I behaved very badly indeed, and that I should have halted our marriage arrangements, but I simply could not face anyone with the truth. My parents were always so delighted about our match that telling them about Henry was very difficult, and as to telling you what I had done, well, that was the most difficult thing of all.

It is because I still feel very deeply about you that I am writing this letter now. I will always love you, Marcus, but it is the love of a very dear friend who prays with all her heart that you will one day be able to forgive her for what she has done.

I know that one day soon you will find someone who will love you as you deserve to be loved, and I hope that when that happens you will be able to think kindly of me again.

Your affectionate and eternal friend,

Constance.

Elizabeth's hands shook a little as she carefully closed the letter again.

Violet waited with almost breathless anticipation. 'Will you go to speak to him in the library, madam?' she blurted at last, unable to bear the suspense.

Tears shimmered in Elizabeth's eyes, and she nodded. 'Yes, I must,' she said softly.

Violet gave a glad smile. 'Oh, madam!'

But as Elizabeth took a candle and left the room to go to the library, she did not know what she would say to him. She had made such dreadful accusations, called him dishonorable and blackguardly, and she had even gone so far as to strike him. . . . When she had conducted herself in such a fashion, it was hardly to be expected that he still wished to turn the clock back to those idyllic and wonderful moments on the terrace that morning.

CHAPTER 18

THE CANDLELIGHT SWAYED over the cornflower-blue of her taffeta gown as she paused by the closed door of the library. Suddenly she was afraid to go in, afraid that all the things she had said were too harsh, and that all he wanted of her now was an apology.

He seemed to know she was there, for he opened the door suddenly, and the light from within flooded over her. He extended an arm to usher her inside.

'Please come in,' he said coolly.

His tone dismayed her, and all her doubts and fears multiplied as she went reluctantly inside.

He closed the door and leaned back against it, his blue eyes as cool as his tone. 'I take it that you have read the letter?'

'Yes.'

'And?'

'And I have been dreadfully wrong.' She could not conceal how her hand shook as she held the letter out to him.

He took the letter and tossed it on to the desk, where it fell close to the miniature of Constance. 'Is that all you have to say, Elizabeth? Simply that you've been dreadfully wrong?'

'I . . . I must ask you to forgive me.'

'And I suppose that I, being a gentleman after all, must be obliged to grant that forgiveness?'

'I do not wish you to feel obliged, sir, for I hope that you will forgive me because you want to.' She was struggling against tears, for more than anything she wanted to fling herself into his arms and beg his forgiveness, beg his kindness, his love. . . .

But he was unbending. 'Perhaps I would want to forgive you, if I felt that you were really sorry for disbelieving me so cruelly in the first place.'

'Cruelly?' Her eyes fled to meet his. 'I . . . I thought that you were deceiving me, that you still loved Constance!'

'Even when I had asked you to be my wife?' He gave an incredulous laugh. 'By God above, Elizabeth, what manner of monster did you take me for?'

She closed her eyes as the tears had their way. 'I loved James, but he was cruel and faithless,' she whispered. 'I thought I loved Alexander, but then I had to face the fact that I did not love him enough, and now he loves Isobel, and I no longer know what is certain and what is not. I love you, Marcus, but I am afraid of being hurt again, for when I am with you I feel as I once did with James, but it all turned so miserably sour before, and now . . .' Her voice trailed away, and the tears wended their way down her cheeks.

'And because it happened before, *ergo* it must happen again?' His voice was no longer cold. 'Oh, Elizabeth, I promise you that this time you may trust your heart, for what I feel for you will never waver. I love you, and I always will.'

Her breath caught, and she took a hesitant step toward

219

him. He relieved her of the candlestick, placing it on the desk, and then he swept her into his arms again, kissing her almost fiercely on the lips.

She pressed close, returning the kiss with such a release of wild emotion that she was oblivious to the library, oblivious to everything except the soaring joy of holding him.

He took her face in his hands, kissing the tears on her cheeks. 'Are all our misunderstandings unraveled now?'

'Yes,' she whispered.

'You know once and for all that I love you and wish to marry you?'

'Yes.'

'Is there anything, anything at all that still makes you anxious?'

'Nothing,' she breathed, her eyes still shining with tears.

'The future is ours?'

'If you wish it,' she said softly.

'Oh, I wish it,' he replied firmly, 'and from now on that is how it will be.' His lips brushed hers again.

She held him, savoring the moment, for she did not wish it to end.

He drew back at last, his eyes dark as they looked into hers. 'We must go to the others, for I fear that Alexander is still in a lather of guilt over you, and will not believe that all is well until he hears it from your own lips. I also fear that Isobel is not entirely at ease, for she knows that she has not conducted herself as a proper young lady should.'

'My own conduct has hardly been beyond reproach.'

'Nor has mine, which means that we all four bear a portion of blame. But since no one has become a loser, and everyone is with the partner of his or her choice, I think that our little cotillion here in the country has been excellently danced, don't you?'

'Our own private *L'Échange*?'

He smiled. 'That is how I see it.'

'There was a time when I was indifferent to that dance, but now . . .'

'Now it will always be a favorite?' he finished for her.

'Yes.'

He drew her palm tenderly to his lips.

Alexander and Isobel were still waiting in the great hall. She was seated on one of the chairs by the long table, and he was pacing nervously up and down. They both turned the moment they heard the others approaching the top of the grand staircase.

Isobel bit her lip anxiously, praying that everything had turned out the way she and Marcus had plotted it would. Alexander hardly dared look, for he could not bear to think that Elizabeth had witnessed how he had finally given in to the irresistible love he now had for her cousin. It did not matter that he had learned that she had formed an attachment for Marcus, for he, Alexander, had not observed her in any misconduct, it only mattered that he had indeed transgressed, and that Elizabeth had seen his fall from grace.

But as Elizabeth and Marcus appeared at the top of the staircase, and those in the hall saw how warmly intimate they were, it was immediately clear that everything had unraveled very satisfactorily indeed.

With a joyful cry, Isobel rose to her feet and hurried toward them as they reached the bottom of the staircase. There she flung her arms around Elizabeth. 'Oh, Elizabeth, I'm so very happy!' she cried a little tearfully.

'And so am I, Isobel,' Elizabeth replied, returning the hug.

Isobel's green eyes became penitent then. 'I'm truly sorry for the way I've behaved. I've been a monstrous brat.'

'It doesn't matter now.'

'But it does. I even fibbed about Father's illness. They don't expect me at Southwell Park, indeed they think I'm still in London. Oh, and when I think of all those crocodile tears I shed in front of poor Aunt Avery, and the way I fainted away in Hyde Park . . .' Isobel pressed her hands to her hot cheeks. 'I don't know what came over me, truly I don't.'

Elizabeth couldn't help a smile. 'Love came over you, that's all.' Then she turned to Alexander, who had lingered uneasily a few feet away. She smiled at him. 'I'm not angry or upset, Alexander, so please do not fear that I bear a grudge. Besides, how could I possibly accuse you when all the time I have been less than honest myself?'

Alexander smiled with relief, running his fingers through his hair. 'All's well that ends well?'

'Yes.'

Marcus took her hand, kissing the fingertips. 'Yes, all's well that ends well, or at least it will be, for we are to be man and wife.'

Isobel turned swiftly to Alexander, slipping her arms coquettishly around his neck and pouting a little. 'You haven't asked me a very important question yet, sir,' she declared.

'An important question?' he replied, his eyes wide and apparently uncomprehending.

'You must ask me to marry you.' She frowned a little crossly. 'Sir Alexander Norrington, must it be left to me? Very well, whether this is a leap year or not, I ask you to do me the inestimable honor of becoming my husband.'

He grinned. 'Well, madam, since you have compromised me beyond all redemption, I suppose must accept.'

'You beast!' she cried, realizing that he had been teasing her. But she laughed with happiness as she raised her lips to meet his.

Elizabeth and Marcus were also lost in each other's arms. She gazed into his eyes. 'I love you, my lord duke,' she whispered.

'I trust you do, Mrs French, for the moment you are my duchess I intend to prove that my kisses so far have not been empty promises.'

His lips were warm and tender over hers, and she could feel the throb of his heart. Then he drew back, his eyes dark with loving desire. 'Madam, I rather think that a special license will be required, and right quickly at that!'